"Don't go back to New York. . . ."

"Don't go," I pleaded, taking her hands in mine. "You could always come live with us."

"Rich, you don't have a spare room."

"So? You could share mine," I teased, making her smile through her tears. "But if your parents didn't buy that, I could name a dozen families that you could live with while you finished high school."

For a second her face looked hopeful. "Really? You think so?" Then she shook her head. "It wouldn't work, Rich. My parents would never go for me living apart from them during my last year at home. You know they're weird that way."

"I can't believe this," I muttered, hearing my own voice crack as I spoke. "What am I going to do without you? Nothing will be the same. Nothing will matter if you're not here. I won't even go to the prom if I can't go with you."

Amber laid her head on my shoulder. "You're so wonderful, Rich," she said softly. "I wish there was a way to keep me here, but I just don't think there is."

Love Stories

Torn Apart

JANET QUIN-HARKIN

BANTAM BOOKS
NEW YORK · TORONTO · LONDON · SYDNEY · AUCKLAND

RL 6, age 12 and up

TORN APART

A Bantam Book / July 1999

Produced by 17th Street Productions,
a division of Daniel Weiss Associates, Inc.
33 West 17th Street, New York, NY 10011.

ISBN: 0-553-49289-6

Published simultaneously in the United States and Canada

Bantam Books are published by Bantam Books, a division of Random
House, Inc. Its trademark, consisting of the words "Bantam Books" and
the portrayal of a rooster, is Registered in U.S. Patent and Trademark
Office and in other countries. Marca Registrada. Bantam Books, 1540
Broadway, New York, New York 10036.

PRINTED IN THE UNITED STATES OF AMERICA

OPM   0 9 8 7 6 5 4 3 2 1

One

Amber

ISN'T IT WEIRD how life-changing days start off like any other day? How there's nothing to warn you of what's to come?

Well, on this particular summer afternoon I was sitting on my front porch, eating a bowl of homemade peach ice cream and reading my mail, when my boyfriend, Rich, showed up. When you live out in the wilds of Wyoming like we do, getting mail is a big deal. You see, we're thirty miles from the nearest movie theater and twenty miles from the nearest pizza place. So mail ranks as a major excitement. Not that I actually get too many letters. I'm partly to blame for that—I'm not exactly the world's greatest letter writer myself. My old friend Suzanne was the only person from my former life in New York City whom I still kept in touch with.

It had been a good mail day for me. I'd just gotten a letter from Suzanne as well as several college catalogs. These were spread out on the bench around me as I heard the sound of a truck coming up the road to our house.

I looked up to see Rich's battered old truck come bouncing over the bumps and potholes. It had been a really harsh winter, and even the paved roads were in poor condition. And the road to our house *wasn't* paved—driving on it now was like driving along a riverbed. But Rich didn't seem to care. He had lived in Wyoming all his life—he was used to these types of things. I, on the other hand, had lived here less than two years. I still wasn't used to ice storms and thunderstorms and rainstorms and forest fires—you name any weather disaster, we got it.

Rich parked his pickup and stepped out. I smiled to myself as I watched him walk toward our house. He was wearing his black cowboy hat as usual, his light brown hair sticking out from under it. He moved with the easy grace of the horses he rode so well. There were times when I couldn't believe how lucky I was to be his girlfriend.

His face lit up when he saw me sitting in the deep shade of the porch. "Hey, Amber," he called. "Just the person I was looking for."

"I should hope so," I teased. "You'd be in big trouble if you were looking for some other girl."

A big grin spread across his face. "Well, I could've come here to talk to your grandpa about the cattle. How's he doing, by the way?"

Grandpa had just had a bad bout of the flu, which had left him feeling pretty weak. "Better," I responded. "He wanted to go out with the tractor this morning, but Dad wouldn't let him. And he was grouching about the way the coffee tasted at breakfast." I smiled. "So that must mean he's back to his old self."

"Good. I was worried about him for a while," Rich admitted.

"I know. Me too. But you know Grandpa. He's as tough as . . ."

"An old boot?" Rich offered, making his way up the porch steps.

I nodded, grinning.

"And as ornery as a grizzly?"

"That too."

"Hi," he said, stepping onto the porch, his eyes gazing deep into mine. He took off his hat and bent down to kiss me.

"Hi," I murmured before our lips met. Then we didn't say anything for a while. After all this time his kisses still knocked all sensible thoughts out of my brain.

"I came to see if you wanted to join me," Rich said as we broke apart. He perched himself on the arm of the bench beside me.

"Join you where?"

"I told you I was thinking about buying a new horse, didn't I?" I nodded and he continued. "Well, I saw this ad in the paper for one yesterday, and I thought I'd go take a look." He handed me the

3

page he'd torn out of our local newspaper.

I glanced down at it. Rich had underlined the words *Palomino stallion for sale. Half broke. Will turn into ideal rodeo horse.*

Half broke. I definitely didn't like the sound of that. "Rich!" I exclaimed, handing the paper back to him. "Are you sure that's the kind of horse you want?"

"Why not?"

"It says half broke, for one thing! That means wild and crazy to me."

"I've broken horses before," he said defensively.

"Really? When?"

"I helped my dad once," he said, running a hand through his thick hair. "I can do it, Amber. And I've always wanted a horse good enough for rodeo work."

Rodeos? I was feeling more uneasy by the second. "Rich—rodeos are dangerous. And I don't want you getting hurt."

Rich shrugged. "I've fallen off a few horses in my life," he told me. "Besides, it's not like I want to be a bull rider or anything. I just want to do calf roping and the stuff I've done since I was a kid." He took my hand in his and squeezed it. "So, are you going to come with me? Or do I have to go see this horse all by myself?"

"Of course I'll come with you," I said, staring into his blue eyes. "But I'm not letting you buy a crazy stallion that's going to kill you."

Rich let out a sigh. "Sometimes you still talk like a city girl," he muttered. "I've been around horses all my life. I know what I'm doing."

4

Rich could be so stubborn sometimes—if he wanted to do something, there was no talking him out of it. "Okay, Mr. Horse Expert," I told him teasingly. "If you wait a second, I'll go get us a snack to bring with us. Mom just baked the greatest raspberry scones."

"She did?" Rich asked suspiciously.

"I know, I know. Beau used to use her scones for target practice. But she's gotten much better. Grandpa even says she bakes as well as Grandma did."

Rich laughed, shaking his head. "I'd say you've all settled in pretty well. You're just like regular Wyoming folks now. I mean, your dad can chop wood without taking his thumb off, your little brother has turned into one tough kid, and your little sister has made friends with all the animals."

I nodded, a smile spreading across my face. "And what talents do *I* have?"

His eyes held mine again. "I could name a lot of things you're good at." He started to lean toward me. I held up my hand to push him away.

"Don't distract me now," I said. "I need to put this stuff inside and grab some scones."

Rich glanced at the mail I was scooping up. "What is all that anyway?"

"College catalogs."

"Oh, yeah. It's getting to that time, isn't it? I guess we *should* start thinking about applying soon." He took one of the brochures from me. "Boston College?" He looked up at me, his eyes opened wide. "Wait a minute. You're thinking of going to school back east?"

"My parents are," I told him. "They wanted me to send away to all these places. I think they want me to get the kind of education they had."

"A lot of good it did them," he said, handing the brochure back to me. "Your mom has her master's and bakes bread. Your dad has a law degree and he spends his time chopping wood, feeding cows, and getting rejection letters for his novel."

I sighed, pushing my red hair away from my face. "Today he got another thanks-but-no-thanks letter from a publisher."

"Pretty depressing, huh?"

I nodded, standing up. "Definitely. He's kind of down these days. In fact, both my parents have been really moody lately. I can tell something's bothering them, but they don't talk about it."

Rich stood up next to me. "Don't worry. I'm sure they'll work it out."

I gave him a small smile. "You're right." I kissed him on his cheek, then said, "I'll be back in a sec."

I ran into the house and dropped the college catalogs on the hall table, catching sight of my face in the hallway mirror. Was this really the same pale-faced girl who'd thought that life didn't exist outside of Manhattan? I took in my healthy tan, my hair that had turned from red to red-blond, the sprinkling of freckles on my nose. And I had muscles on my arms too—I'd definitely lifted enough bales of hay during the past two years. Who needed a gym?

I grinned to myself. "Looking good," I told my reflection. Then I ran into the kitchen and snatched a couple of raspberry scones from the cooling rack. Nobody was around except Grandpa, who was still in bed upstairs. Mom had taken Katie to the store, and Beau was helping Dad with the cattle.

Rich had the truck door open for me when I came outside. I climbed in, handing him a scone. Then he started the truck and we bumped along the road until it met the highway.

Half an hour later we pulled up outside an old ranch property out in the scrublands to the east.

"Okay, remember we're just looking," I warned him before we got out of the car. "Don't get carried away and buy a horse that you're not going to be able to break."

"No, ma'am," Rich teased, flashing me a grin.

"I'm only saying this because I know what you're like," I said. "Remember that leather jacket you bought because you thought it looked so good in the store? It was so tight on you that you couldn't even lift your arms, and it's still hanging in your closet."

Rich shook his head. "I won't get carried away by looks."

"All right," I said, not sure that I really believed him.

We both hopped out of the truck. Before we reached the main house we had to walk by a corral, and standing in it was the most beautiful horse I had ever seen in my life. Its blond coat looked as if it was made of spun gold and its mane, streaming out in the wind, was a pure silver color.

"Oh, wow," I said, forgetting everything I'd just

said. "He's totally beautiful, Rich. Look at that tail."

"Yeah," Rich agreed. "I bet he's fast too. Check out those muscles."

"Are you the boy who called about Sultan?" a voice behind us asked. We both turned to see an old man walking toward us from the direction of the barn. "Real pretty, ain't he?" the man went on. "Good price too. Want to try him out?"

Rich nodded and smiled. "Definitely."

I watched nervously as Rich and the owner tried to saddle Sultan. It wasn't easy.

"He'll get used to it. It'll just take a while," the owner explained as Sultan danced and reared and I yelled out, "Rich, be careful," about a hundred times. Sultan did behave okay once Rich was on his back, but that wild gleam in the horse's eyes still made me uncomfortable.

Rich spent a little while longer with Sultan and then talked to the owner for a few minutes about prices. Was Rich actually serious about this horse?

As soon as we were in the truck and headed back home, I had my chance to find out. "So, are you really thinking of getting him?" I asked. *Please say no, please say no,* I pleaded inwardly.

"You bet," he told me.

My heart dropped—I knew there was no way he'd change his mind now.

"He's asking a great price, and I made a good profit from my calves this year. I'm going to bring my dad out to take a look, but if he thinks Sultan is a good investment, then I'm going to go for it."

"I hope you know what you're doing," I said. "He's a beautiful horse, but he's still pretty wild."

"Pretty and wild," Rich said, taking his eyes off the road to flash me a wicked smile. "That's how I like my women too—hey, don't hit me when I'm driving," he added, laughing, after I punched him.

"Well, then don't make sexist comments." I laughed along with him. I settled back into my seat. "Anyway, it's going to take a lot of work to get him broken. You'll have to ride him every day, won't you?"

"Probably."

"Do you really think you'll have time, Rich? I mean, we're going to be seniors. A lot's going to be happening. You know how hard the coach works you—and this year you're the best receiver on the team. Plus student council . . ."

"No problem," Rich responded. "I'll just get you to ride Sultan when I'm too busy."

"Me? You think *I* could ride that horse?"

"Sure, why not? You're turning into a great rider."

"Well, I'm going to be busy too, you know," I said, secretly pleased that Rich thought I was good enough to ride such a wild horse. "I want to take the cheerleading team to the state finals this year. And don't forget, I'm on student council too."

"*And* you'll probably be homecoming queen," Rich said, taking his eyes off the road once more to smile at me.

I blushed, feeling a great surge of excitement. Me, homecoming queen? I knew it was possible. I was definitely one of the leading contenders.

I looked out the truck window and smiled to my-self as I thought about how my friend Suzanne in New York would laugh herself silly if she knew that things like being homecoming queen mattered to me. But they did. I'd come to love the way that old-fashioned school spirit still existed in Wyoming. I loved cheering at football games, riding down main street in parades, and getting dressed up for formal school dances. In fact, I just loved being here, period. I realized now that coming to Wyoming was the smartest thing my family had ever done.

"Well, maybe I'll let you escort me to home-coming. *If* you behave yourself," I said playfully, turning back to look at Rich. "For once I can't wait for school to start."

"Amber, you're not seriously going back east to college, are you?" Rich blurted out suddenly. "I thought we said we'd try to go to the same school."

"I haven't really thought about it yet," I said, caught off guard. *Has he been thinking about this ever since we left my house?* I wondered. "I mean, the catalogs just arrived today. But I can tell my parents would like me to go to a good school."

"There are good schools out here too," Rich said defensively. "And an elite eastern college is no use to *me*. I don't need to know about the kings and queens of Europe or whether van Gogh painted the *Mona Lisa*."

I hit him again. "You know as well as I do that he didn't. Stop trying to play the farm boy."

He grinned. "You get what I'm saying, though,

don't you? I'm going to take over the ranch some-day. I need to know about soil preservation and cattle management—things that are going to be useful to me. And I don't think they offer those kind of courses at East Coast schools."

"They do at some of them," I said. "I know that Cornell has an agricultural school, for example."

"Cornell?" Rich repeated. "What are the odds that I'll get in there? That we'll both be accepted there?"

"You're right," I mumbled. I stared out the window. We'd talked about going to college to-gether, but we hadn't given it any serious thought until now. I tried to imagine me in Boston or New York and Rich out west. Then I shook my head. There was no way I'd want to be apart from him for four whole years.

He must have been sharing my thoughts because he touched my knee gently and said, "There are plenty of good schools out here. We'll figure some-thing out. And we've got an entire senior year to have fun together first."

"That's right," I agreed, grabbing onto his hand. "I wonder where I'll have to go to find a cool dress for the senior prom? Maybe we can drive into Denver. . . ."

"Why not fly to Beverly Hills?" Rich teased.

We turned into my driveway, bouncing and lurching up to the house.

"Maybe I'll come and take a look at those catalogs." Rich laughed, switching the gear into neutral. "I might want to change my mind about being a rancher. Maybe I'll take modern dance and sculpture at Harvard instead."

"You're terrible." I laughed too, climbing down from the truck.

"Well, do you know what you'll want to major in?" he asked as we walked up to my house together.

"No. I haven't thought about it too much." I shrugged. "I don't even know what I want to do with my life."

"A rancher's wife isn't a bad career choice," he joked as we made our way up the porch steps. "Although you have to make sure you lasso yourself a real cute rancher."

"Are there any?" I quipped back.

We were still laughing and jostling each other when we burst into the living room. Five worried faces looked up at us.

I stopped in the doorway. "What is it?" I asked, glancing from my parents to my grandfather to my brother and sister.

"We were waiting for you to come back," Mom said. "Sit down, Amber. Grandpa's got something to say to us."

Rich stepped back. "I guess I should be going," he said. "See ya, Amber. I'll let you know about the horse."

Nobody stopped him. That's how I knew the conversation was going to be serious. I mean, Rich was almost like family—he was always welcome.

I heard his truck door slam and the engine start up.

"Sit down, honey," Grandpa said, clearing his

throat. "What I've got to say isn't going to be easy."

Crazy thoughts started to race through my head. Had I done something wrong? Were my parents getting a divorce? What could all this seriousness be about?

"I had a talk with Dr. Chambers the other day," Grandpa began. "He said I've made good progress and gotten over the flu pretty well, but he told me that I have to stop thinking that I can still run a ranch. And I shouldn't be spending another winter in this climate."

There was complete silence in the room. I think we were all holding our breath. I could hear the deep, even tick of the clock in the hall and a couple of sparrows chittering to each other outside.

"I wrote to my old friend Charlie Hayes," Grandpa went on. "He had to move to Arizona for health reasons a few years back. I got a letter from him today. He tells me that I'm welcome to come and spend the winter with him, and that's what I plan to do."

"But what will happen to the ranch, Grandpa?" Beau blurted out. "Dad's still useless with cattle. We can't run it by ourselves."

Grandpa smiled a tired sort of smile. "You're right, Beau. Your dad is still useless with cattle."

"I wouldn't say useless," Dad put in.

"We would," the rest of us said at the same time.

"Okay, so cows and I don't get along," Dad relented. "But I guess we could muddle through somehow."

13

Grandpa shook his head. "No, you can't. I've decided to sell the herd."

Move to Arizona? Sell the herd? My brain could barely process what I was hearing. How could this be happening? What would we do?

"What will you do for money, Grandpa?" Beau asked. It was amazing the way my eleven-year-old little brother asked all the questions the rest of us wanted to but were too scared to say out loud. "And we don't make any money," Beau went on. "I'm not old enough yet. And Dad hasn't sold his books."

"Mom could sell her biscuits and jam," Katie suggested.

"I don't think we'd make too much that way, sweetie." My mom smiled sadly. Katie was pretty mature for six and a half years old, but she still didn't get how complicated life could be.

Dad cleared his throat. "I think Grandpa's decision forces us all to see the truth," he said, exchanging a knowing look with my mother. "I'm never going to be a rancher," he told us. "Maybe you kids can run this place someday, but not me. And it looks like I'm never going to be a novelist either. Your mom and I didn't want to tell you this before because we thought you were all so happy here, but my old law firm wants me back. They've called several times. I've been seriously considering it."

Mom spoke next. "And I could probably go back to my old ad agency . . . or find work at another one. To tell you guys the truth, part of me misses working."

14

"So, that's settled, then," Grandpa said, clapping. "You take the kids back to New York, and I'll live on the money I get from renting out this place."

It was as if time stood still, the world stopped turning, and the sun went out as this awful news finally sank into my brain.

"Wait a second!" I yelled. "You can't be serious! You can't want us to move back to New York! Not now. Not me. No way!"

Two

Rich

I FELT KIND of weird all the way home. I shivered as I drove, even though it was a hot, sticky August day.

Something was very wrong over at Amber's house. One look at their faces and I could tell I wasn't wanted there. Any other time her grandpa would have said, "Sit down, boy. We've got no secrets from you." But this time he was quiet, and nobody stopped me from leaving—not even Amber.

I began to wonder if it was anything I'd done. Were they mad at me for something? I'd always treated Amber well, hadn't I? I'd never gotten her home too late after we'd been out on dates. No, it had nothing to do with me, I realized. I just wished I knew what it was all about.

I parked my truck in the shade of the big pine

tree and headed for my house. On my way there, I caught sight of my mom out back, picking tomatoes, and I remembered about the horse I'd just seen. The awkward situation at Amber's had forced him completely out of my mind.

"Hey, Mom. Is Dad around?" I called to her.

"Hi, honey." She smiled and straightened up, shielding her eyes from the sun as she talked to me. "No, he went with Jeb to fix fences over in the top pasture. He'll be back for dinner."

"Oh, okay."

I must have looked disappointed because Mom frowned. "Did you need him for something urgent?" she asked.

"Well, I wanted to see if he had time to go look at a horse with me."

"Another horse?" Mom asked, raising her eyebrows. "Don't we have enough horses on this property?"

"Mom, this one would be for me," I explained. "All we've got here are steady old ranch horses. They're no use if I want to rodeo."

Mom put her hands on her hips, her face growing worried. "I don't want you entering rodeos. You could get hurt."

I grinned. She sounded just like Amber. "I'll be careful," I promised. "I just want a good horse that I can finish breaking myself."

Mom wiped her hands on her apron. The pockets were already bulging with tomatoes. "Rich, are you sure you'll have time to take on an extra responsibility?" she asked. "You have to put in a lot of hard work if you want to get into a good college. You've been pretty much goofing off all through high school."

"I have not!" I protested, even though she was partly right—I hadn't worked as hard as I could have. "Anyway, Coach says I might get offered a football scholarship."

"You need to concentrate on academics," Mom argued. "Football's not going to get you anywhere in life. And didn't you say that you and Amber want to go to the same college?" I nodded. "Then you better get serious about school," she continued. "Amber's very smart, and she studies a lot."

"I know." I scuffed the toe of my boot into the grass. "Actually, I think I should go call her in a minute," I said. "Something weird was going on at her house."

"Weird? What do you mean?"

"I'm not really sure," I said. "But when we got back to her house, her whole family was just sitting there, looking worried. And they didn't want me around."

"Maybe they had some bad news. A death in the family?"

I shook my head. "They wouldn't have minded sharing that with me. I think I'll go call her now." I turned and started for the house.

"Rich, hold off for a while," Mom called after me. "Give Amber time to call you. If it is bad news of some kind, she might need to be alone first.

She'll tell you her news when she's ready."

"I guess you're right," I said, although I was itching with impatience. "Maybe I'll saddle up Bonnie and go see if I can track down Dad. . . ."

The phone rang. "That's Amber!" I yelled, and sprinted into the house.

"Hi, babe, what's up?" I said breathlessly as I picked up the receiver.

"Rich. I need you. Something terrible's happened." Amber was sobbing so hard that I could barely understand what she was saying.

"I'll be right over," I said, my heart dropping to my boots at the sadness in her voice. "Hang in there, baby. I'll see you in a minute." I hung up the phone without even asking her what the terrible thing was. If Amber needed me, I wasn't going to make her wait a second longer than she needed to.

I drove like a madman, my hat hitting against the truck roof as I took the potholes way too fast. Amber was waiting by the gate when I came up her driveway. I opened the truck door, and she climbed in. Her face was streaked with tears.

"Oh, Rich," she cried, throwing herself into my arms.

"What is it?" I asked, panicked. I could feel her shaking against my body.

"We're leaving," she sobbed. "We're going back to New York."

What? I held her away from me so that I could look into her eyes. "Back to New York? Are you serious? Why? I thought you all loved it here."

She took a deep breath, obviously trying to control her tears. "The doctor told Grandpa that he has to spend the winter somewhere warm for health reasons. And Grandpa doesn't think my dad can run the ranch alone."

"I could help," I volunteered desperately. "I'd come over after school every day like I did when your grandpa broke his leg. We'd manage okay."

Amber shook her head so violently that I was sprayed with her tears. "You don't understand. Grandpa needs to rent out the ranch for money. And my parents actually *want* to go back to New York. It turns out that they've been thinking about it for some time now, but they didn't want to leave Grandpa alone."

"They want to go back there?" I asked, hardly believing that we were really having this conversation. How could they take Amber away from me?

"My dad's been offered his old job back," Amber said. She had quieted down and wasn't crying anymore. "And my mom doesn't think she'll have a problem finding one. She even said that she misses working."

"I see," I mumbled. I didn't know what else to say. I felt like someone had punched me in the gut and all the wind was knocked out of me. "What about you?" I asked at last. "Do you want to go?"

"Of course I don't." Amber started to cry again. "Do you really think I'd want to leave you? And you know how I was looking forward to senior year. We were going to win the state championship.

I might've been homecoming queen. I was going to go to the prom with you. And now it's never going to happen. None of it."

"Then don't go," I pleaded, taking her hands in mine. "You could always come live with us."

"Rich, you don't have a spare room."

"So? You could share mine," I teased, making her smile through her tears. "But if your parents didn't buy that, I could name a dozen families that you could live with while you finished high school."

For a second her face looked hopeful. "Really? You think so?" Then she shook her head. "It wouldn't work, Rich. My parents would never go for me living apart from them during my last year at home. You know they're weird that way."

"I can't believe this," I muttered, hearing my own voice crack as I spoke. "What am I going to do without you? Nothing will be the same. Nothing will matter if you're not here. I won't even go to the prom if I can't go with you."

Amber laid her head on my shoulder. "You're so wonderful, Rich," she said softly. "I wish there was a way to keep me here, but I just don't think there is."

After that afternoon, every day that followed was like living in a nightmare. I kept hoping to wake up and discover that it wasn't true, that Amber wasn't really leaving. But she was. One day a moving truck came to move most of their stuff, and I had to walk away—I just couldn't bear to watch.

I tried to spend every minute with Amber, but

when I was with her, I didn't always know what to say to make her feel better. And it wasn't easy being in Amber's house. Her little brother and sister didn't want to leave any more than she did. It would be an understatement to say that there was a lot of fighting going on in that household. But her parents had made up their minds—they were moving back to New York, and that was that.

I brought Amber with me when I went to buy the horse. I wanted to at least share that with her before she left, even though she still wasn't too happy about my buying him.

"Are you sure you know what you're doing?" she asked me as we finally got Sultan into the horse trailer after a lot of bucking and kicking. "He looks very wild to me. Mean too."

"Don't worry. I'll be careful," I said, getting into the truck. "Anyway, I've got lots of time to work with him now that I don't have you around to distract me."

"So that's what I was to you, a distraction?" She said it in a teasing tone, but I heard her voice tremble.

I took her into my arms. "You were my whole life," I told her. "And you still are. Without you nothing matters. I'm just going to keep myself busy until I get to be with you again."

"We'll make it somehow, won't we?" Amber asked, pulling away and looking up at me. "We will get to be together again, right?"

"Sure, we will. We said we'd go to the same college—nothing's changed about that. And if you decide to go to one of those schools back east, no problem. I'll be the only farm boy at Harvard."

"Oh, Rich." She was laughing now, her eyes sparkling. "I can't imagine life without you."

"I know. Me either." I started the engine and drove off slowly so that I didn't freak Sultan out. "But it's only a year apart. We'll survive," I said, trying to reassure myself as much as I was trying to reassure her. "Long-distance relationships can work if the two people care enough about each other, and we definitely do. We'll write every day. We'll call each other. You can come back here for one vacation, then I'll come out to you the next. It'll be over in a flash."

"I hope so," she said, cuddling into me.

I squeezed her tight. I hoped so too.

After that afternoon time seemed to move at warp speed. It was like being on a roller coaster, going faster and faster and not being able to stop it no matter what. I'd say to myself, "In two more days she'll be gone," then, "In one more day she'll be gone." Then one horrible morning I woke up and the voice inside me said, "Amber leaves today."

When I went over to her house, the car was packed up and ready to go. She was standing on the porch, just staring out into space. She didn't even move as I came up the steps.

"I'm trying to burn this scene into my mind so I'll never forget it, ever," she said. "I thought it would be like living at the end of the earth when I first got here. Now it seems like paradise."

23

I walked up to her and stroked her thick, red-blond hair. "You'll be back," I told her. "Your grandpa's only planning on spending the winter away. You'll be out here next summer. I'll have Sultan broke and whipped into shape by then. You can come and cheer me when I win all those rodeo blue ribbons."

"Is that all you want me back here for—a cheering section?" she asked, a little smile crossing her face.

"You know why I want you back here," I said.

She looked around. "Let's go for a walk," she suggested. "They won't be ready to leave for a good half hour yet. Let's go down by the stream."

"Okay." I took her hand—it felt so warm and comfortable and right in mine. We went behind the house, past the corral and the sheds, following the shady path down to the stream. We'd been there a million times together—I tried to remember each one of those times now. We'd sat in the shade of that one tree and studied for our finals together last spring. We'd taken a picnic and gone swimming when the river was running higher and . . .

"That's where you put that frog down my back," Amber reminded me suddenly. "Remember? I was sitting on that rock and you put a frog down my back, you jerk."

"I was five years old, Amber. Give me a break," I said, grinning. It was the first time I'd met her. She'd come to visit her grandpa, and I'd thought she was the prettiest thing I'd ever seen. "Besides, I

24

only did it to show that I liked you," I told her. "I had to find some way to get your attention."

"You sure got it," she said. "That totally freaked me out."

"I remember." I smiled at that memory—Amber jumped and squirmed and yelled like she was being killed or something, and everyone came running at once.

"It was a weird way to show you liked me," she commented, perching herself on the same rock she'd sat on years earlier and staring down at the swiftly flowing water.

"Well, I guess I couldn't find the right words to say what you meant to me," I said. "I still can't. I can never explain to you what you've meant to me this past year and a half, Amber. Or how I'm going to—" I broke off and turned away. I didn't want Amber to see me crying.

She slid down from the rock and wrapped her arms around my neck. "It'll be okay, Rich. It will all work out somehow," she promised. "Nothing's stronger than love, is it? If we love each other, then nothing can pull us apart. Nothing."

I squeezed her closer to me and we just stood there, wrapped tightly in each other's arms, my cheek against her soft hair, until we became aware that people were yelling her name.

"I guess you have to go," I said, letting her out of my arms.

"Guess so," she said softly. She looked around, a small smile playing across her lips. "Maybe they'll never find us and they'll leave without me."

"Hey, that's a thought." I grinned. "We could run away and live up in the cabin where we got snowed in that New Year's."

"Rich, get serious."

"It would work," I said. "I'd take my hunting rifle and shoot us food. I'd kill us a big old grizzly, and you could skin it, and we'd eat the meat, and you could make us coats out of the skin. . . ." I looked at her expression of disbelief and laughed. "I guess not, huh?"

"It's a lovely dream," she said. "Maybe it'll happen someday—well, except for the part about me skinning the bear—but right now I have to go."

I took her hand again, and we walked back along the narrow trail.

"I wish I had something to give you to show you how important you are to me," I told her. "I've been looking, but you know what the stores are like around here. There was nothing special enough."

"You've already given me something special," she said. "You've given me your heart."

The rest of her family was already standing by the car with her grandfather when we got there. Katie was rushing around hugging every animal in sight. "Bye, Lammie. Be good," she said, hugging a big sheep she'd adopted as a little lamb. "Have fun at Kim's house." She'd found families to adopt all of her critters.

"Bye, Grandpa," Beau said, trying hard to act

like he didn't care. "I'll write and tell you about my new school. I'm going to take karate lessons too."

"You don't need karate, son," Amber's grandpa said, grabbing Beau's arm. "You've got Wyoming muscles now. You can take on any New Yorker without karate." He ruffled Beau's hair, and Beau climbed hastily into the car.

"Get in, honey, we have to get going. We've got a lot of miles to do today," Amber's father said. He took my hand and shook it. "So long, Rich. Thanks for taking such good care of Amber. She's had a great time here."

I didn't want to open my mouth because I wasn't sure I could control my voice. I just nodded.

Amber's mom gave me a peck on the cheek. "Bye, Rich. Take care. We'll talk to you soon." Then she got into the car as well.

Amber reached up and kissed me gently on the lips. "Good-bye, Rich," she said. "I love you."

"I love you too," I whispered, kissing her hair as she moved away from me.

And then I just watched. The car door slammed. The engine started. Amber's grandpa came to stand beside me.

"Drive safely," he called to his family. "Give me a call when you get there. Take care of yourselves."

"We will, Grandpa," Amber called back. "You take care too. Have fun in Arizona."

The car moved off. Hands waved from all the windows. Amber's dad tooted the horn. I felt like a statue. It was almost impossible to lift my arm to wave back. But I forced myself to. I kept on waving as the car disappeared around the bend and there was nothing left but a cloud of dust.

Amber's grandpa put his hand on my shoulder. "I guess they've really gone, son," he said in a broken voice. "Now it's just you and me again."

Three

Amber

"HOME AT LAST," my father announced as he turned the key in the door of our old apartment on Fifth Avenue. It was three days later, and we were all hot, tired, and in serious need of showers.

I stepped into the living room. I'd forgotten how small and empty looking it was. One wall was floor-to-ceiling glass. Outside the window the lights of the city were twinkling beyond the blackness of Central Park. There was a white carpet on the floor, and the furniture was all black and white, glass and chrome—very modern. That had been my parents' taste when they'd furnished this place. I had thought it looked pretty cool before. Now I just thought it looked cold. The air-conditioning was going full blast, and I shivered.

"This place is like a deep freeze," I said.

"I asked the janitor to get the air-conditioning going before we arrived," Dad explained. The tenants who were subletting this place while we were in Wyoming moved out a couple of months ago. "I figured it would be pretty stuffy in here. You know what New York in the summer can be like."

"The balcony!" Katie exclaimed, rushing over to the window. "Mom, I could keep a rabbit out here, couldn't I? Or a very small lamb?"

"No pets allowed, I'm afraid, honey," Mom said. "We could get you a tank of fish, though, or maybe a turtle?"

"I don't want a dumb tank of fish!" Katie yelled. "You can't hug fish. I want Lammie. I want to go home!" She burst into tears and rushed out of the room.

I ran after her. I knew just how she felt. After all, I was feeling the same way. But it had to be even more confusing for Katie, who had been too young when we'd moved to remember much about life in a big city.

I found her sitting on the bed in her old room. "It's okay, Katie. It's going to be okay," I lied as I sat on the bed beside her and slipped my arm around her shoulders.

"No, it's not," she whined. "I hate it here. This doesn't even look like my room."

"We'll make it like your room," I promised. "We'll go out tomorrow and get animal posters and a fuzzy blanket and anything else you want."

30

Mom came in and helped Katie get undressed. I walked into my old room, knowing exactly what Katie meant. It didn't feel like my room at all. No homemade quilt on my bed. No funky old furniture. And I couldn't see mountains when I looked out the window. But nobody came in to tell *me* it was going to be okay. Probably because they knew it wasn't going to be.

I took a long, hot shower and climbed into bed. There was my old Slimline phone beside my bed. I dialed Rich's number.

"I'm back in New York," I said when he answered.

"Glad you got home safely."

"It doesn't feel like home. It feels like a cold, empty place, far away from you."

"Hang in there, babe," Rich said. "You're tough. You can get through this. Just promise me one thing."

"What?"

"That you won't start liking New York so much that you forget about me."

"As if I could, silly. I'm going to hate every moment until I'm with you again."

After I'd hung up, Mom came into my room. "I made you some hot chocolate so that you can sleep," she said. When I didn't answer, she sat down on my bed. "Amber, honey, I know you're mad at us now, but we had to do what we thought was best for everybody. And in terms of money, we just couldn't stay in Wyoming. The offer your dad got to go back to his old company was just too good to turn down, and this new ad agency I'm starting with is giving me a great salary too." She picked up one of my pillows and hugged it. "Besides, you might actually be more excited by your choice of classes here. There's more to school here than home ec and cheerleading."

"It wasn't like that at Indian Valley!" I said angrily, staring out at the sea of twinkling lights. "I took all college-prep classes. And you were the one who forced me to leave New York, remember? You thought all the kids at Dover were spoiled."

"You're right," Mom agreed. "But now that you've seen a whole different way of life, we don't have to worry about you being influenced by kids who have too much money and freedom. You have real values now. And in any case, the bottom line is that we don't have a choice. So you might as well enjoy yourself while you're here." She touched my forehead, brushing some strands of hair away from my face. "You have a bright future ahead of you, honey. And you have to be realistic too. That future might not include Rich."

"What?" I sat up straight. "Of course it will include Rich. What are you talking about?"

She gave me one of those annoying mother-knows-best smiles. "You'll both be growing up and changing during these next few years. You'll date a lot of guys before you find the one for keeps. Rich is a nice boy, but——"

"But what?" I demanded. "He's only a Wyoming farm boy?"

"I didn't mean that. I just meant that your futures

could go in very different directions. I don't want you to shut yourself off from having fun just because Rich's not around anymore. New York can be rough, but it's an exciting place. I want you to make the most of it."

She kissed me on the forehead and walked out.

"Yeah. Right," I growled to myself as I pulled the covers over my head.

It was impossible to get to sleep that night. Sirens wailed, planes roared overhead, and cars honked. How was I ever going to be able to sleep with all that noise?

But I guess I must have drifted off eventually because soon I was dreaming that the phone was ringing, and I knew it was Rich, but I couldn't lift myself out of bed to talk to him. Then the next moment I opened my eyes and realized that the door buzzer was buzzing—in real life. And then I heard my dad call, "Amber, it's Suzanne. She's on her way up."

It might have been late morning in New York, but I was still on Wyoming time. "Why is she here so early?" I grumbled, getting up and pulling on shorts and an Indian Valley sweatshirt. I just had time to brush my hair before Suzanne burst into my room, smiling brightly.

I blinked back at her, surprised at how different she looked. Suzanne was dressed as if she was attending a business meeting or a modeling session— long black dress, heavy silver necklace, high black clogs, and lots of makeup. Her hair, which I remembered as being long, dark brown, and curly, was now jet black and cropped into a bob. Before I could finish reacting to this glamorous vision, she threw open her arms and rushed across the room to me.

"Amber!" she yelled loud enough for all of Manhattan to hear. "I can't believe it! You're back! And look at you—you're so tanned and gorgeous! Who did the streaks in your hair? They look amazing."

"The sun, Suzanne," I said, laughing as she hugged me. "It's what you get when you help with hay making."

"Well, it looks great. You look just great, really. I'm so happy to see you!"

I smiled back at her. "So am I," I told her. New York might be the last place I wanted to be, but I *was* happy to see my old friend Suzanne.

"Come on," she said, tugging on my arm. "I'm taking you out for bagels. I have to remind you of all the great things you've been missing."

Before I knew it, we were out in the bright sunlight of the city sidewalks, zillions of people streaming past us. I couldn't believe how crowded the streets seemed. *How did I ever like living here?* I wondered as we waited to cross the street, taking in all the bustle surrounding me. Drivers honked, diesel fumes belched, and lights flashed on and off. At 8 A.M. Wyoming time, it was a little much to take.

The light changed to green, and I started to

34

walk. Suzanne grabbed me, pulling me back. "Are you crazy? You almost got hit by that taxi!"

"But the light was green."

She laughed. "How long have you been away? This is New York, Amber. Taxis don't obey stoplights—you know that." She shook her head. "I think I'm going to have to teach you Survival 101."

That's a fact, I thought miserably as we crossed the street. *I sure don't know how I'm going to survive living here.*

Ten minutes later we were sitting in The Bagelry. I stared like an idiot at the menu—which was three pages long. Were there really that many different ways to serve bagels? In Wyoming the menus listed simple items—like steak, hamburgers, or grilled cheese. The nearest restaurant that served breakfast was twenty miles away—and they only served the traditional meal of bacon, sausage, eggs, and hash browns. You'd never see a spinach bagel with sun-dried tomato cream cheese on *their* menu.

The waiter came to the table to take our order. I still had no clue as to what I wanted, so I motioned to Suzanne to order first.

"I'll have a sesame bagel with low-fat dill cream cheese and tomato," she told the waiter. "And a double mocha with nonfat whip and a sprinkle of cinnamon."

She might have been speaking Swahili as far as I was concerned. Had *I* sounded like that two years ago? Had I known what all this stuff was?

"I'll have, um, scrambled eggs and bacon on a bagel," I said. "And some orange juice."

"Bacon?" Suzanne looked horrified. "Think of the nitrates and the cholesterol. Not to mention the fat."

"In Wyoming *everyone* eats bacon. And they all live long lives. My grandpa is almost eighty-two."

Suzanne shrugged. "I guess they burn off the calories with all that hay tossing and cattle chasing," she said. "But remember, you don't come from there, Amber. You come from here. I mean, Wyoming was just a minor blip on the landscape of your life—I'm planning to be a writer, did I tell you that? Well, I'm really into images right now. And I'm so excited about the creative-writing class I've signed up for. You got my letter telling you about my courses, didn't you?"

She hardly gave me time to nod before she went on. *Did she always talk so fast?* I thought, barely able to keep up.

"There was so much to choose from," she continued. "I just couldn't decide. I really wanted to do advanced theater, but I had to be practical and go with physics. The good colleges all want you to have a strong science background, don't they, even if you're into arts?"

She paused, looking at me, and I realized that she was actually giving me a chance to respond. "I don't know," I told her. "I haven't really checked into all that yet."

Suzanne's big brown eyes opened even wider. "But it's almost time to send off applications! Haven't you thought about what you're going to say in your essays? I mean, they have to be really original, or the schools won't accept you." She collected her breath for a short moment as the waiter placed our food in front of us. Then she went on, "I took an application-essay writing class in summer school—to practice. For my personal statement, I think I'll compare my mission to be a writer to the first landing on the moon."

I was beginning to feel like *I'd* just landed on the moon. *An application-essay writing class?* Was she for real? All I could do was sip my orange juice and stare back at Suzanne stupidly.

"Anyway, I'm taking you to Fiorelli's tonight," she continued. "Remember Fiorelli's—the coffee shop where we used to hang out? I've called everyone. The whole gang's going to be there."

I took a bite of my eggs, unsure if I was prepared to see the "whole gang" yet. Suzanne and The Bagelry were enough for me to handle at the moment. Then I had a sudden thought. "Is Brendan going to be there?" I asked, cringing. There was no way I wanted to see Brendan yet—or maybe ever. He had been my first real boyfriend. Before Rich.

"Brendan? He transferred out of Dover Prep—didn't I tell you?" Suzanne asked. "He's really into basketball now. He wants to go out for a basketball scholarship, and he'd have no chance of that playing for our pathetic team. If he'd wanted a dance scholarship or a flute scholarship, that'd be another story." She carefully placed a big slice of tomato on top of her bagel. "Will you be into theater again, do you think?"

"I don't know," I said, shrugging. I couldn't

imagine being into *anything* again at the moment. *If only I could go back to Wyoming and be with Rich,* I thought, picking at my bagel. It hadn't even been a full week, and already I missed him like crazy.

Suzanne didn't seem to be aware of my miserable mood. "You know what?" she asked excitedly, her face lighting up. "We could go shopping! No offense, but your whole wardrobe must be out of date."

"My whole wardrobe is shorts and jeans," I said. "And most of my jeans smell of horse, but I'll have to live with that until I get a job. My parents are kind of tight with money right now." My mom had told me that the whole family would have to live no-frills for a while since most of my parents' money was going toward paying for private school for Katie, Beau, and me.

"Oh," Suzanne responded, taking a sip of her mocha and looking like she was at a rare loss for words. Then she said, "Wait—you're planning on working during senior year? Amber, how will you fit it in? You need extracurricular activities on your college applications. I'm sure you didn't do much in Wyoming."

"I was captain of cheerleading," I said.

She shook her head, smiling. "Somehow I don't think that's going to impress NYU."

"Well, I probably won't be going to NYU. Rich and I want to go to the same school. For his sake, we need to choose a place that has ranch-management classes."

Suzanne wrinkled her little button of a nose.

"You're going to go to a cow college? Amber, get real. Rich was a great guy to date while you were out there, but there are plenty of guys in New York. You'll move on."

I could feel my cheeks flame up in anger, but I told myself to calm down. How could Suzanne know how much Rich meant to me? I'd never really explained it to her. Besides, I wasn't in the mood for an argument. I just wanted to go home and go to bed. "Not in a million years," I told her simply. "I'll never break up with Rich."

Suzanne's response was to roll her eyes.

As we walked back from the bagel place, I let Suzanne do most of the talking. I was too busy thinking. How could we have been best friends once? I wondered. Now it seemed like we were on different planets. Would I become like her if I lived in New York for a while? Did I want to be like her?

Oh, Rich, I thought, staring up at the tall buildings. *I wish you were here. I wish you'd ride up on your gold-and-silver horse and whisk me away from all this!*

I really didn't want to go to Fiorelli's that night. If I found Suzanne overwhelming, how was I going to handle a table full of Suzannes? But Suzanne wasn't the kind of person to take no for an answer. "Of course you're coming," she'd insisted. "You can't be jet-lagged—you didn't even fly. And anyway, it's all arranged."

It was easier to give in than to fight. All that emotion had left me feeling tired and drained.

What did it matter if I met people or not? I didn't even care.

The moment I stepped inside Fiorelli's, memories came rushing back to me. The opera posters on the walls, the aromatic smell of roasting coffee, the classical music playing, and the two guys in the corner concentrating on their chess game—it all felt so familiar. After all, I'd spent a major portion of my life here once. It had been my main hangout.

"Amber! There she is!" voices yelled from a corner table. Hands were waving crazily. I recognized Thomas, Mandy (with a new hair color), Alicia, looking very sophisticated, and Suzanne—all my old clique, crammed into a corner booth. I had to admit, part of me was slightly excited to see them all.

"Hi, guys." I smiled, sliding into the seat beside Suzanne.

"Here she is, Miss Dairy Queen!" Thomas declared.

"It wasn't dairy—it was cattle!" Mandy corrected.

"Sorry, Miss Ranch Queen, then. What kind of queens do they have out there, Amber?"

Oh, boy. Any excitement I had felt disappeared at their teasing. I was just not in the mood. "Well," I told them, "we have rodeo queens. And a homecoming queen at school."

"Homecoming queen! They still go for that sexist junk?" Suzanne laughed. "Can you imagine if we had a homecoming queen at Dover?"

"It wouldn't be you, Suzanne. Your legs aren't sexy enough," Thomas joked.

I shifted in my seat uncomfortably. I *knew* this

was how they'd react. Why'd I even bring it up? To torture myself?

"That's exactly what I mean," Suzanne said. "Those things give girls the wrong message—that outer beauty is all that matters."

"Homecoming queen's not just about beauty," I said defensively. "It's judged on personality too."

"It's still a popularity contest," Suzanne argued. "I'm so glad that Dover doesn't go for superficial things like that."

I wanted to tell Suzanne that Indian Valley wasn't what she thought it was. The girls who got chosen for homecoming queen were the ones with the most school spirit, not the most popular. But I knew it would be pointless to argue—Suzanne wouldn't be impressed with school spirit either. She could be so close-minded.

"Well, anyway, I'm glad you're back, Amber." Alicia smiled at me and tossed back her long hair. "I don't know how you survived so long in the wilderness. It was very brave of you."

"I didn't have to hunt buffalo or anything, Alicia," I responded. "I actually really loved living in Wyoming."

"Oh," Alicia said, nodding. "I see." Then she looked at me as if I'd just said I liked living in the sewers or something.

I glanced around the table at my old friends, feeling my cheeks getting very hot. Who were these people?

I kept very quiet for the rest of the evening while

they talked about plays I hadn't seen and people I didn't know. Had these people really once been my friends?

The worst part was, I could tell they felt sorry for me. I hated that—as if having lived in Wyoming was equivalent to having had some sort of a disease.

I couldn't have been more happy than I was when we all stood up to leave. At that moment Suzanne said, "I'd better walk Amber home. She'll probably get mugged or something."

"I'd like to see someone try to mug me," I told her. "I've wrestled steers—I've got muscles."

Wrong thing to say again. They all burst out laughing at me.

The second I got home, I called Rich. "I don't think I can take it here," I told him. "I feel like I'm from another planet, Rich." Then I told him about my conversation with my former friends.

"It's going to take a while, babe," he said after I'd finished. "Just like it took a while for you to settle in here. But you're a strong person. You can handle it. Just promise me one thing."

"What's that?" I asked, already feeling better after having heard his voice.

"Don't go trying to wrestle any muggers," he said playfully. Then in a more serious voice he added, "Be safe, Amber. New York's a dangerous place."

"Don't you worry about me," I responded, twirling the phone cord around my finger. "Besides, I won't be going anywhere anyway. I'll just be going to school, doing homework, and counting down the days until I can be with you again."

Four

Rich

I STOOD HOLDING the receiver for a long time after Amber had hung up. I'd tried to seem positive for her sake, but inside I was scared.

Muggers? Where had that thought come from? I hadn't thought about the dangers of Amber being in a big city. I'd just been upset that she was so far away. Now I had a new thing to worry about. I'd told her that she was strong and she could handle things, but could she, really? If I could just see her, see that she was okay in New York . . . Somehow I had to find time to get a job—one that paid enough money so that I could buy a plane ticket to New York City.

"Do you know anyone who's looking for a hired hand?" I asked my dad at dinner that night.

"Who wants work?" he asked, taking the basket of biscuits my mom handed him.

"Me."

"You? Why would you want to go work for other people?" he demanded, frowning at me. "If you've got time on your hands, I could use a little more help around the ranch. Those fences up toward the ridge need a lot of work."

I sighed, shaking my head. "But Dad, I need to make money so that I can pay for my plane fare to visit Amber."

He gave me a knowing smile. I hated when he did that. "Let her be. Amber's a great girl, but she's far away now. There are plenty of other girls out there, you know. Don't keep fretting over something you can't have."

"Who says I can't have her?" I snapped. "Amber and I—we're meant for each other. And I'm not going to give up on her. Ever." I got up from the table, fuming.

"Where are you going?" Mom asked.

"Out. I'm not hungry."

I stomped away, not wanting to face them for another second. They'd never understand—my mom acting like life was going on as normal, my dad's smug smile. He thought that I was just a kid and that Amber was just some girl. I'd soon get over her—right! Would the earth get over it if the sun went out?

I opened the back door and stepped into the yard. It was almost dark there in the shadow of the mountains. My feet crunched on the gravel as I headed toward the corral behind the tractor shed to visit Sultan. He whinnied when he heard me coming. Walking over to him,

I reached out my hand to stroke his face. But he threw back his head and skittered away, looking like a crazy golden shadow running across the corral.

"What am I going to do with you?" I muttered, watching him. What on earth had possessed me to buy him? Amber was right—he was too wild. I didn't even know if I wanted to bother trying to break him properly. And if I sold him right now, I'd have almost enough for the plane fare to see Amber. Then a new thought popped into my mind: If I put the effort into breaking him and making him into a good riding horse, then I could sell him for a whole heap of money.

"Okay, Sultan," I said to him. "The schoolin' starts tomorrow. I'm going to New York . . . and you're my ticket there."

But it turned out I was all talk. The next day I had other things to keep me busy. I'd promised Amber's grandfather that I'd help him pack up and leave for Arizona. I really didn't want to go over to that house so soon after Amber had left it, but a promise was a promise. And besides, the old man was like my own grandpa.

"Well, hi, there, Rich," he greeted me as I jumped out of the truck. He was on his way to the barn with a load of household items.

"I'm locking all this away," he called to me. "I don't want strangers messing with my personal things."

I ran over to grab hold of a lamp that was about to slip from his hands. "When are they getting here?" I asked, walking with him into the barn.

"This weekend. I'd appreciate it if you'd keep an eye on the place for me, Rich. They sounded like nice enough folks on the phone, but you never can tell." He put his armload of stuff on the floor. "I'd hate to come back to find my place wrecked."

"I'd never let that happen, Mr. Stevens," I promised, placing the lamp down. "I'll watch the house for you."

"Fine. I'm not sure what these people know about ranching," he said as we headed out into the bright sunlight again. "The man told me they'd lived on a ranch before, but they've been in Denver for a while. They might need advice if they're planning to run cattle."

"Okay," I said. "Sure."

"And I'd really appreciate it if you'd go welcome them for me, make sure they know where everything is and see that they get settled in."

I nodded silently. Did he know what he was asking me to do? Did he know how hard it would be for me to go inside a house that held so many memories?

But I wanted to do all I could for Mr. Stevens. It couldn't be easy for him to give up this home that he'd lived in all his life.

Just as I was thinking that, Amber's grandpa suddenly stopped in place halfway across the yard and just stood there, looking around.

"Is something wrong?" I asked.

"It's just sinking in that I won't be seeing this place again," he told me. "At least for a while."

46

"The winter will go fast. You'll be back next summer." I put my hand on his shoulder—something I'd never dared do before.

"Right," he replied, shaking his head and starting to walk again. "Stupid old fool. I'm getting sentimental in my old age. Now, come and help me carry out my bags to the car and then we'll have a bite to eat together."

"Sounds good to me," I said.

Fifteen minutes later we were sitting on his porch, sharing some cheese and apples and strong black coffee—just the way he liked it.

"You heard from Amber yet?" he asked me.

"Twice since she got to New York."

"I've only spoken to her parents. How's she doing?"

"She's pretty depressed," I told him. "It's all kind of overwhelming for her."

He touched my arm lightly. "I want you to do something for me, Rich," he said. "I want you to keep an eye on her for me."

"I don't see how I can do that when I'm here and she's clear across the country," I responded.

His pressure on my arm grew stronger. "Don't let her get wrapped up in New York life. You keep her tied to this place, you hear me?"

"But I don't see how—," I started to say again.

He cut me off. "Don't let her slip away from you. You hold on to what's important in life, Rich. Fight for her if you have to."

I nodded, staring into the old man's brown eyes. "Don't worry. I intend to."

He smiled weakly. "I like to think that you and her will live in this house someday when I'm gone. She's like her grandma, you know."

I just looked back at him, unable to say a word. He had never spoken to me like this before, with so much emotion.

He brushed a tear from his eye and stood up. "I better get moving," he said. We chucked our apple cores across the yard and brought our coffee mugs inside, where I washed them in the sink. Then we walked back outside. He whistled for Jack, the puppy that Amber had given him a couple of years ago, now a fine, full-grown border collie. "Let's get going, boy," he called.

He took a last look around the property. Then he locked the front door and walked over to the car.

"I'll be seein' ya, Mr. Stevens," I called to him.

"I hope so, Rich," he said.

For the second time that week I stood there waving good-bye as a car disappeared into a cloud of dust.

On Sunday I decided to do what Amber's grandpa had asked of me—to welcome the new family to his house. We'd heard that they'd arrived during the night. There's not much that gets by people in a small town like mine.

I figured that this might also be a good opportunity for me to start my work with Sultan—I could ride him over to the house.

It took me half an hour to get him saddled, and

then my dad had to come and help me tighten the girth. When I got on top of him, he danced around awhile at first, but then I took him across the pasture, gave him his head and let him run, which he liked. So he'd had a lot of the friskiness knocked out of him by the time I rode up to the Stevenses' place.

A dog rushed out of the house, barking furiously. Then a girl followed him. She was petite with light hair, and as she stood there, in the deep shadow of the porch, my heart did a huge flip-flop. For a second I thought I was looking at Amber!

She came back to surprise me! I swung myself down from the horse, my heart pounding.

But then I crashed back down to reality. The girl stepped out of the shadows, and I saw that she wasn't Amber at all. She was a girl I'd never seen before—thin and pretty, wearing jeans and a checked shirt, her hair lighter than Amber's and in a braid down her back.

"If you're looking for the Stevenses, they've gone," she said. Her voice wasn't soft like Amber's was.

"I know. Mr. Stevens asked me to come over and make sure that you've settled in okay," I explained. "I'm Rich Winters. We have the spread about half a mile down the road, where the big poplar trees are."

The girl walked toward me. "Hi, there. Melanie Turner," she said, shaking my hand. "Pleased to meet you." Her grip was firm, like a guy's.

"Well, welcome to Indian Valley, Melanie. I hope you like it here."

"I'm not too sure about that," she responded, glancing down at the ground. "Moving here wasn't my idea. I was happy where I was. And I'm not looking forward to my senior year at a new high school either."

"Don't worry, you'll fit in right away," I told her. "Amber did."

She lifted an eyebrow. "Amber?"

"Amber Stevens—Mr. Stevens's granddaughter. The girl who lived in this house before you. She moved here from New York, and man, it was a shock for her at first. But she ended up loving it here and . . ." My voice gave out on me. I couldn't go on talking about Amber like she was a character in a book and not someone I knew. Someone I loved.

Melanie's eyes searched my face. "Your girl-friend?" she asked.

I nodded.

"Where'd she move to?"

"Back to New York," I told her.

"That's gotta be tough on you," she said.

I cleared my throat. I wanted to change the subject before I did something really dumb, like cry. "Anyway. So how are you all settling in here?" I glanced around the property and spotted a man over by the shed, trying to get Grandpa's old tractor started. "If you need any help, just ask. That tractor's kind of temperamental. And I see you've got horses. If you need any pointers on how to handle them—"

At that moment the tractor backfired. Sultan reared up, his hooves flailing at the air. The reins slipped from my hands, and before I knew it, he was off, dancing around the yard with the stirrups flying, trying to buck off his saddle.

Melanie didn't hesitate for a second. She ran after him.

"Watch out!" I yelled after her. "He's only half broke. You could get yourself—"

I broke off midsentence.

"Easy, boy," Melanie was saying. She had her hand on Sultan's flank and then on his forehead. And the whole time he just stood there, gentle as a lamb.

Melanie looked over at me and grinned. "Now, what were you saying about giving me pointers on horses?"

Five

Amber

WHEN I OPENED my eyes Tuesday morning, I felt my insides twist themselves into knots. For a moment I couldn't think why. Then it hit me. Today was my first day back at Dover.

The knots in my stomach wouldn't go away as I got out of bed and showered. I had to admit it *was* great having my own bathroom again after having shared one between the six of us. And having a centrally heated apartment wasn't bad either. But these were only minor things. I'd willingly have stood in line for the bathroom forever and ever if it was a bathroom in Indian Valley, near Rich.

I wish you were here, I whispered to Rich's photo that I'd placed beside my bed.

But he wasn't. And I had to deal with getting ready for school. I had been up for hours the night before, agonizing over what to wear. The clothes that had been fashionable before I left New York were now totally out. Finally I'd decided on a long black skirt with little yellow flowers and a black tank top.

Suzanne came by early to pick me up. At least it was nice that she was so excited for me to come back to Dover. I really needed a friend right now, even if I wasn't sure that the two of us had enough in common anymore.

"You look great, Amber," she said when she walked into my apartment.

"So do you." Suzanne looked fabulous as usual. She wore a soft purple shirt with black figures all over it and a long, flowing gauze skirt.

"Really? Do you like this shirt? It's hand embroidered from Pakistan," Suzanne said.

"Yes, it's nice." Then I called to my brother and sister, "Good luck, guys." They were starting at their old school today as well.

"I'm going to need it," Beau responded, rolling his eyes. "I bet Tony Mancini is there, waiting to take my lunch money again."

"You can take Tony Mancini," I said, giving him an encouraging smile. "You've got muscles now."

"You're right," he said, and he smiled too.

Twenty minutes later I felt like a new freshman as I walked up the steps and into the Dover building with Suzanne. I would have liked to slip inside quietly, but I had Suzanne with me—my very own PR person.

"Hey, everybody, guess what? Amber's back!" she yelled to everyone she knew. "You remember

Amber? She went to live in the boonies, and now she's back."

Oh, boy. How am I going to make it through today? I smiled weakly as strange faces stared back at me.

Alicia, Mandy, and Thomas were waiting for Suzanne and me by the lockers they had saved for us.

"It's so cool being a senior." Alicia beamed. "We get first choice of lockers. I kicked two sophomores out of these for you two."

"Thanks," I said, not sure of how to respond. I didn't care which locker was mine—they all pretty much looked the same to me.

"So, let's see your schedule, Amber," Thomas said. I handed it to him, and he studied it. "Great. You've got old Hansen with me for math. He's good."

"But tough," Alicia added, peering over Thomas's shoulder. "He gives a ton of homework."

"So does Rosenberg for honors English," Mandy added, pointing to his name on my schedule. "He makes you read, like, a book a week. This girl I knew in his class said she never got to bed before midnight."

"Great," I muttered. Not that I planned to have an active social life or anything, but how would I find the time to get a part-time job if I had hours of homework every day?

Just one more perk of moving to New York, I thought as we all walked down the hall to our first-period classes.

★   ★   ★

54

At lunchtime we had an activities fair—all of the various clubs had booths in the auditorium, trying to recruit new members.

"So, what are we going to sign up for?" Suzanne asked, linking arms with me. "Let's see what turns us on: computer club? Nah, too nerdy. Aerobics club? Nah, too, uh, aerobic."

I had to laugh. Suzanne might be different from me, but she *was* funny.

"Art club," she continued. "That would be okay *if* I could draw, which I can't. Street hockey—now, there's a thought."

"You can't be serious!" I exclaimed. I couldn't imagine elegant, dainty Suzanne as a killer machine on blades.

She grinned. "Of course I'm not serious. When have you ever known me to be serious? Go on, you pick something we both can do."

"I don't know, Suzanne," I told her. "I'm not sure I've got time for any of this. Have you seen my schedule? All of my teachers so far have told me that I'll have tons of reading and homework. And I really want to get a job too. That's the only way I'll have enough money to buy a ticket back to Wyoming."

Suzanne squeezed my arm. "Relax and stop worrying," she said. "Your parents have gone back to their old jobs, right?" I nodded. "Okay, so they may not have money now, but by winter vacation they'll have enough to fly you out there. If not, you'll put in a couple of weeks working at Macy's or Bloomies before the holidays."

I hadn't thought about it that way. "Maybe you're right."

"Of course I am. If not, I'll lend you the money."

I blinked back at her, touched by her generosity. "Really?"

"Yes." She smiled and nodded. "Anyway, you have to get involved in extracurricular activities. It looks good on your applications. *And* it could be fun. So pick something already."

I looked at the overwhelming cluster of booths. I'd just come from a school where Future Farmers and cheerleading were about the only after-school options.

"Well," I began, "we need to narrow it down. We only want something that will look great on applications—not take up too much time."

At that moment Suzanne squealed, dragging me across the room. "Quest ended," she announced. "This is what we're going to do." She gestured at the poster announcing auditions for the fall musical.

I'd been in a Dover Prep production before. It was about as close to Broadway as you could get—they really took the arts seriously. "Oh, no, Suzanne," I said. "Not the school musical. I was in *West Side Story* my freshman year, remember? I was only in a couple of dance numbers, but it was brutal—rehearsals every night. I don't have time for that."

Suzanne pouted. She is the only person I know who can get away with a pout and still look beautiful. "But it will be such fun," she said, her brown eyes pleading. "We don't have to go out for big parts. We'll just be in the chorus—we probably wouldn't get leads if we wanted them anyway. There are some really talented actors at this school." She looked around and poked me in the side. "See her?" she whispered, focusing on a beautiful blond girl standing close to me. "That's Bailey Blakely. She was in a revival of *Annie* on Broadway."

"Tryouts soon, Bailey," someone called to the girl. She tossed her luxurious mane of hair around, almost hitting me in the face.

"Tryouts?" she asked, laughing. "You mean we have to try out with everyone else? Don't be ridiculous."

It was a case of hate at first sight. For one thing, I hate people who have long, heavy hair that they flip into people's faces. And for another, I hate snobs.

"That settles it, Suzanne," I said. "There's no way I'd be in a play with her."

"Come on, Amber. For me. Please? Pretty please?" Suzanne did the famous pout again, her eyes opening wide.

"I'll come along to auditions with you," I told her. "Just to keep you company. Then I'll see how I feel about things."

"Great! You'll see—we'll be in the chorus together. It'll be so cool." Suzanne smiled. "Hey, let's practice. Ready? One and two and . . ." She tried to do a Rockettes routine, kicking up her legs in her long, tight skirt. She almost fell flat on her butt.

I couldn't stop giggling as I watched her. Suddenly it hit me that I'd missed having a girl-friend I could really laugh with—or at. The girls at

Indian Valley had been very friendly, but they would never willingly make fun of themselves in public—not like Suzanne. It had never really dawned on me before, but their sense of humor had been very different from mine.

Maybe I *could* get through this year with Suzanne by my side.

I waited impatiently for Rich to get home from school that evening, which wouldn't be until about six o'clock my time. My parents had given me a limit on my long-distance phone calls, so I looked forward to every call I'd budgeted for myself the way kids look forward to summer vacation. I should have been getting down to the homework my teachers had already given me, but I kept staring at the clock until at last it was time, and I grabbed the phone.

"How was your first day?" he asked before I could ask him.

"Overwhelming," I said. I had so much to tell him! "I have such hard classes, Rich. All my teachers expect a ton of reading and written assignments, and my English teacher wants us to keep a daily journal as well. I don't see how I'm going to be able to get a job, and Suzanne wants me to try out for the musical with her—"

"You should," Rich put in encouragingly. "You're a great dancer—you'd be terrific in a musical. Remember how good you were as Rudolph the Red-Nosed Reindeer in that Christmas skit?"

"Rich, kids at Dover have performed on

Broadway," I told him. "They won't be impressed by my Rudolph performance."

"Don't you go putting yourself down, Amber. You're as talented as anyone at that school. And you can handle anything. You learned how to drive a tractor out here. And you learned how to ~~toss hay~~ and feed cattle and ride a horse. . . ."

I had to laugh. "I don't think that driving tractors or riding horses is that exciting to anyone in New York. But speaking of horses, how is Sultan coming along?"

"He's, uh, okay."

The tone of his voice had me worried. "What? Is he difficult to work with?"

"You could say that. He made me look like a total fool the other day. I went over to welcome the family that moved into your house, just like I'd promised your grandpa I would, and I'm standing talking to this girl when the old tractor backfires and Sultan takes off on me. Worse still, the girl goes after him, puts her hand on him, and he goes with her, no problem."

"Huh. How about that," I said. *Girl* was the word that was echoing around my head. *This girl.* "So—a new girl has moved into our house?"

"Yup. You should see her, Amber," he said. "She's amazing with horses. It's incredible. And she's tiny too. Not even as tall as you."

I could hear the admiration in his voice, and it made my stomach turn. I wanted to ask how old she was and if she was pretty, but I didn't. I just

59

couldn't find a way to get the words out without sounding jealous. Which I was.

After we'd hung up, I tried to concentrate on my government textbook, but I couldn't. I knew that Rich would never cheat on me with another girl.

He wouldn't. Would he?

Six

Rich

IN A WAY I was glad that Amber hadn't asked me how my first days back at school had gone because they hadn't been too great. In fact, I'd felt like a big, black cloud had settled over me, just like the thunderclouds that brought storms to Indian Valley that time of year. I kept telling myself that this was my senior year—my year of triumph. I was going to be the big man on campus. I'd waited three whole years for this, but now that it was here, I didn't even care.

"What's with you, man?" Chuck Harris asked me as we walked back to the locker room after football practice one afternoon.

"Nothing—why?"

"You weren't listening when Coach was giving that new play to us. You ran the wrong pattern."

I shook my head as I opened my locker. "Sorry. My mind was on other things."

"Amber?" Chuck guessed. "You're still thinking about her?"

I sighed. "I just can't get her out of my mind, Chuck. Nothing seems to matter now that she's not here."

"You're gonna have to get over her, Rich," Chuck told me, putting a friendly hand on my shoulder as I sat down on the bench. "Coach is not the kind of guy who'd understand that you flubbed a pass because of some girl."

"Not just *some girl*," I corrected. "My girl." I looked up at Chuck. "We were both looking forward to this year. So many great things were supposed to happen—"

"They still can," Chuck interrupted, sitting down next to me. "Life doesn't have to end because she moved away, you know. We've got a whole football season ahead of us. Don't blow your chances because she's not here."

"I'm trying not to," I said, running a hand through my hair. "But it's hard. You don't understand."

"You're right—I don't," Chuck agreed. He stood back up and opened his locker. "Face it, Rich. She's gone—it's time to move on. And you could have any girl you want in this school. The moment they heard that Amber was out of here, they were all lining up to date you."

I stared back at him—it was useless. He'd never comprehend how important Amber was to me.

"Yeah, well, I'm not interested," I muttered.

"Not interested in what?" Wayne Beardsley asked, coming out of nowhere and flopping down beside me. "Man, that was a brutal workout. I ache all over."

"He's not interested in seeing another girl," Chuck responded for me.

Wayne's eyebrows shot up. "You're going to go girl-less your whole senior year?" He gave me a punch that nearly knocked me off the bench. "Get outta here, Winters. What about homecoming, huh? And parties with the cheerleaders? You mean to tell me you're going to stay home and watch TV while the rest of the team is out partying?"

I shrugged. "I'll still go to the parties," I told him. "I'm just not going to get involved with anyone. Amber and I promised each other."

Wayne rolled his eyes. *"Amber and I promised each other,"* he mimicked. "Man, you sound like an old married guy. You're seventeen, Rich. You're supposed to be out there having fun. You don't want to be tied down to one girl yet. I know I don't intend to be."

I shook my head, frustrated. It was beyond pointless to argue with Wayne. He was the biggest pig around.

"You've never been tied down to a girl for more than a week, Wayne," Mike Morris quipped, flicking him with his towel as he went past.

"So? I get bored quickly," Wayne said.

"Either that or they do." Mike gave me a wink. "A week's about all they can stand of your company."

"You're just jealous, Morris, because you

63

haven't got my great body," Wayne said, getting up and towering over Mike.

"Great bodies might get girls," Mike commented, "but unfortunately they usually like some kind of a brain to go along with it."

This was the usual kind of kidding around that went on in the locker room. In the past I'd have been right in the middle of it, wisecracking with the other guys. Now I couldn't think of anything to say. My brain was too crowded with thoughts of Amber.

"Hey, Winters, what about that new girl who just moved into the Stevenses' place?" Mike asked me, pulling me back into the conversation. "She's kinda cute, isn't she?"

"Yeah, what's her name—Melody something?" Wayne added.

"Melanie," I answered quietly. "Melanie Turner."

"You should go for it, Winters," Chuck said, giving me a dig in the ribs. "She must be lonely, not knowing anybody around here. She's your neighbor, isn't she? And we were taught in Sunday school to be friendly to our neighbors. Ask her out."

"Just leave me alone, guys," I told them, standing up. I threw my helmet into my locker. "I'm not in the market, okay? Go do your own shopping!"

Then I shoved Wayne out of the way and stomped out of the locker room. I heard Mike's voice ask, "What's eating him these days?"

I didn't wait around to hear the answer.

*　　　*　　　*

That Friday we had our first game of the season, against the Cody Mustangs, our big rivals. People in Indian Valley take their football seriously, so every seat in the bleachers was filled. And it looked as if every single resident of Cody had driven forty miles to cheer on their team as well. As we were about to run onto the field, Coach called me over to him.

"Winters, get focused, okay?" he said. "This is an important game for us. Don't let your teammates down."

"Don't worry, Coach. I'll do my job," I promised.

"I hope so," he said, looking hard at me. "Sometimes I get the feeling you don't care anymore. I've got someone waiting to take your starting slot if you don't want it. Now get out there and play hard, you hear me?"

I nodded silently, feeling chills go down my spine at Coach's words. I'd been the starting wide receiver on the team since my sophomore year. This year everyone expected me to be the star.

"That's Rich Winters," I'd heard freshmen whispering to each other in the halls behind me at school. "You know, the football player."

I had to show Coach that I hadn't lost my edge tonight.

The game started. Cody was a tough team—they had a lot of really big guys, and they played great defense. By the end of the first half I was sore and bruised from the punishing tackles I'd taken. We were tied at fourteen when we came out after half-time. For a long while nobody scored. Both defenses held. Then, with only five minutes left in the game, Cody scored a field goal. The air was thick with tension. We didn't have much time left, and we needed another touchdown or a field goal to win.

Coach called the new play. I had to run deep up the middle, then cut left. I broke free of the corner-back who was guarding me, sprinted like crazy down the field, and cut left, just like we'd practiced. The ball came flying through the air just ahead of me, perfectly thrown. I could sense the goal line ahead. I was going to score the winning touchdown!

The ball dropped into my outstretched hands.

I wish Amber could see this! The thought just popped into my mind out of nowhere, and along with it an image of her appeared, jumping up and down and cheering for me, the way she always did.

Suddenly—*crunch*. I was hit from behind and felt the ball fly from my hands. I felt my shoulder hit the turf. There were groans from all over the field, and the announcer yelled, "Fumble!"

I couldn't look my teammates or Coach in the eye as I walked back to the bench. Next play he sent a junior in my place. And then he didn't say a word to me as we walked off the field. We'd just lost 17–14. *I'd* just lost it for us. The day Amber drove away had been the worst day of my life. This one came in a close second.

Feeling like my body was made out of lead, I walked up to Coach. "I'm sorry," I told him. "I won't let it happen again."

He had this unnerving way of staring as if he

could see right inside you. "You know, Winters, what I'm not happy about is that you're making me look like a fool," he said. "All summer long at coaches' meetings, you know what I was doing? I was bragging about this wide receiver I had who was going to run circles around everybody and never dropped the ball. How do you think I feel now?"

"As bad as I do," I responded, dropping my head. "Look, Coach, I'm going through a bad time right now. My girlfriend went away a couple of weeks ago—"

"Your girlfriend?" he exploded. "This is all about a dumb girl?"

"She's not a dumb girl!" I exploded back at him, my cheeks flaming up.

He placed a big hand on my shoulder. "Forget about her, Winters. No woman is worth wrecking your chances for. I had you down as scholarship material. I've invited scouts from big-name colleges to come and watch you play. You want me to call them and tell them not to come after all?"

"No, sir," I mumbled, looking down at my feet.

"Then get with the program, boy," Coach ordered, squeezing my shoulder hard where it already hurt from the tackle. "You want your starting slot back, you have to show me what you can do. And if I don't see one hundred and ten percent effort from you at practice, I'll call those scouts and tell them not to waste their time. Do I make myself clear?"

"Yes, sir," I muttered.

"Go home, take a bath, and soak that shoulder,"

Coach said. "You won't be of any use if you stiffen up. Go on, get out of here."

I didn't need to be told twice—I got out of there. I slipped away from the field without going back into the locker room. I couldn't face the guys, I felt low enough as it was.

A lot of the crowd had gone, but there were still plenty of cars in the parking lot. At least my parents had gone to visit relatives out of town for the weekend and had missed my horrible playing. I slunk to my truck, hoping nobody would notice me.

What was happening to me? What had happened to that guy who was going to be the big man on campus, the football star?

I have to have something left, I thought, opening my car door. If I lost football, I'd have nothing at all. No scholarship, no good school . . . and then I wouldn't get to be with Amber next year.

That thought really woke me up. What if Amber got into great schools and I had to go to the local junior college? Then we'd never be together again, ever!

Sitting in my truck, I made a vow that I'd give football everything I had. I'd work like crazy, I'd concentrate, and I'd show Coach who was scholarship material!

Seven

Amber

I REALLY DIDN'T want to go to auditions on Friday. The night before, I'd fallen asleep right in the middle of doing my homework. If I was going to be this tired trying to get all of my work done, how would I ever be able to handle rehearsals as well? Nobody knew what the musical was going to be, but there was a rumor that it was *Grease*. And there was no way that I felt like being bright and perky in front of a hundred Dover Prep students. I wouldn't have even gone if Suzanne hadn't literally dragged me there.

"Suzanne, this is dumb," I said as we walked into an auditorium that was already full to overflowing. "Look at all these people."

Some of the girls were wearing leotards and had their hair up in buns, like professional ballet dancers.

There were even a couple of *guys* in leotards. I could just picture Rich's face if he'd been there. "I'm outta here," he'd whisper to me. "There's no way anybody's ever going to get me to wear tights." I smiled at the thought and wished he were here with me, holding my hand. I'd have tried out for the New York City Ballet if Rich was beside me. Who was I kidding? I'd have tried out to be the lion tamer in the circus just to have Rich by my side again.

"It's only going to be embarrassing," I continued to mutter to Suzanne, who was busy pushing her way through the crowd.

"Baloney. They need a chorus, don't they? You and I can high kick with the best of them."

"Not in long, tight skirts," I pointed out. We were both wearing them today.

"We'll do fine. Don't be such a killjoy," Suzanne teased, giving me a friendly shove. "What's with you? This could be fun. Remember what fun we had in *West Side Story*? Remember the cast parties and staying up until two in the morning to finish painting the set? Remember when the guy who played Bernardo got his pants caught on the wire fence and ripped them?"

I grinned—I'd forgotten all those things. It was weird—it was almost like those memories belonged to someone else's life, not mine.

"You see," Suzanne said triumphantly, seeing my smile. "You do remember." She shook her head. "Why do I feel like a character in a soap opera—you know, when the heroine has amnesia and they're trying to make her remember the guy she was engaged to before he marries someone called Cheetah or—"

"Bailey?" I suggested, glancing over at the snobby blond actress.

"Amber! Naughty, naughty." Suzanne giggled. "I like it!"

We were both laughing as we squeezed into two empty seats. "You know, you should go for one of the comedy speaking parts," I told Suzanne. "You're really funny. If it is *Grease,* go for Rizzo."

"Has your amnesia blocked out the way I sing?" she asked, her brown eyes opened wide with surprise. "It hasn't improved in the past two years. I'll be quite happy to be a chorus dancer, thank you." Then she nudged me. "Looks like we're gonna start soon."

Mr. Peters, the theater-arts teacher, was walking through the front doors. I watched as he took a seat at a table that had been set up for him. A couple of senior girls with clipboards stood behind him, just like on a film set. The noise level dropped to hushed whispers.

Bailey and her friends pushed some freshmen out of the seats in front of us and sat down as well. "The only question," Bailey said, loudly enough for half the auditorium to hear, "is whether I'm innocent enough to play Sandy."

This was apparently a joke because her friends laughed. "And I'm really bummed out that we're doing *Grease,*" she went on. "All those years of voice training and I don't get to show off what I can

71

do. I mean, I took that whole summer program with the Met—and for what? *'You're the one that I want—ooh, ooh, ooh,'"* she sang in a little voice. At least, she probably thought it was little. But it echoed around the room.

I leaned into Suzanne. "Are there any musicals with no female leads at all—or one in which the female lead is old and ugly?"

Suzanne got my meaning and giggled. "That's not nice," she said. "And Bailey *is* talented. Unfortunately she knows it."

"Listen up, everybody," Mr. Peters suddenly boomed in a big voice. "First of all—welcome. It's very good of you all to come when you don't even know what you're trying out for. The reason we didn't announce the play on the posters was that we've just changed our minds."

"Thank God," Bailey whispered loudly. "Maybe now we get to do *Phantom of the Opera* or something that really shows off my voice."

I rolled my eyes. Did she ever shut up? She was so full of herself.

"We had planned to do *Grease* this year," Mr. Peters continued. "But we have just received a very generous grant from one of the school's benefactors—a Mr. Homer Tidesdale from Texas. Mr. Tidesdale has given us enough money to hire a professional set designer and a Broadway choreographer. He has also promised to build us a completely new theater—"

"Wow!" kids around me exclaimed. Some people applauded.

72

"Well, you can express your thanks in person," Mr. Peters went on, glancing nervously at the door, "because the principal is bringing him to join us any moment now. He wanted to sit in on auditions."

Bailey beamed. "That guy is a multibillionaire," she said. "Maybe he'll finance my own show after he's heard me sing."

"So before he gets here," Mr. Peters said, "I wanted to tell you that he didn't like the idea of *Grease*. He has requested that we do *his* favorite musical—*Annie Get Your Gun*."

There was stunned silence, then someone said, "What?"

Mr. Peters cleared his throat, an unpleasant expression on his face. Obviously he wasn't too happy about directing *Annie Get Your Gun* either. "It was a big hit back in the fifties," he said. "It's about Annie Oakley, who's a sharpshooter with a famous Wild West show. You've probably heard some of the numbers: 'You Can't Get a Man with a Gun'? 'Anything You Can Do, I Can Do Better'?"

There was still stunned silence. Apparently nobody in that room had ever seen *Annie Get Your Gun*—except me.

"I know those songs," I whispered to Suzanne.

She raised an eyebrow.

"They did it over at Cody High. We went to watch. It was cute."

Bailey didn't think so. "*Annie Get Your Gun*?" she whined. "Tell me this is a bad dream."

At that moment the doors opened again and the

principal came in, accompanied by a big, jolly-looking man wearing a cowboy hat—the kind of hat that everyone wore back in Indian Valley. But here in New York he looked like a character from, well, *Annie Get Your Gun*.

"Ladies and gentlemen, this is Mr. Tidesdale," Principal Edwards said. "I hope you'll make him very welcome." She pulled out a chair, motioning for Mr. Tidesdale to sit.

"Welcome, Mr. Tidesdale." Mr. Peters glanced nervously at him. Then he cleared his throat again. "Okay. We're going to start with a cold reading," he announced. "Then we'll learn some of the numbers together. Bailey—would you come up here and read Annie? Sean—would you read Wild Bill?"

A tall, slim guy who bore a remarkable resemblance to Leonardo DiCaprio stood up.

"That's Sean O'Brien. Isn't he gorgeous?" Suzanne whispered.

I nodded.

Mr. Peters called out some more names.

"I don't know why they bother to have tryouts," Suzanne whispered. "They've got all the leads precast—look who he's calling out now. I mean, what chance does any girl have of getting Annie when Bailey's tried out for it first?"

"I can't say that Bailey is my idea of the Wild West," I commented, watching her. I tried to imagine her in jeans and a checked shirt, like what everyone wore in Indian Valley. I also tried to imagine her on a horse. . . . But then, I didn't suppose that even

74

Mr. Tidesdale would spring for real horses.

"Okay, act one, scene one. Begin," Mr. Peters cued.

They started reading. I sat there, only half listening until they really began to get on my nerves. Their accents sounded ridiculous. "That's not how people talk out west," I whispered to Suzanne. "They're making it sound like the Beverly Hillbillies."

Suzanne just shrugged.

I sat there, my face flushing bright red, as I got madder and madder. Did they really think that everyone outside of New York sounded like a hick?

When Bailey was supposed to look like she was throwing a lasso, I couldn't stand it any longer. I burst out laughing. The actors stopped in their places. Mr. Peters looked up.

"What was that about?" he asked. "If there's something funny, would you mind sharing it?"

I got to my feet. "I'm sorry, but they've got it all wrong," I blurted out, unable to hold it in. "Those accents—that's not how people talk at all."

Suddenly I could feel a hundred pairs of eyes staring at me. I felt very self-conscious, but I also knew I was right.

"And you're an expert, are you?" Mr. Peters asked sarcastically. He gazed at me for a moment. "I don't think I know you."

"Amber Stevens," I told him. "I've just moved back here from Wyoming, and no real cowboy talks like that, trust me. And when she pretended to throw a lasso—well, sorry, I laughed."

"Then you'd better come down here and show us how it's done," Mr. Peters said.

"Um, okay."

Suzanne grabbed my hand and squeezed it.

I swallowed hard, but I climbed onto the stage and walked out to where the other actors were. I could feel Bailey glaring at me.

"You don't twirl over your head like that," I explained. "You'd never rope cattle that way."

I could hear some chuckles from the audience—and some particularly loud ones from Bailey—but I didn't care. "So, you just do this." I demonstrated the lassoing motions. I wished they'd had a real lasso rope there. I'd have loved to lasso Bailey.

When I was finished demonstrating, I said, "And the accents are all wrong too."

"I was thinking the same thing myself," Mr. Tidesdale said, nodding at me. "Why don't you read a couple of speeches and let them hear a good western accent?"

I gave him a small smile. "I'd be happy to." I glanced over at Mr. Peters, and he motioned for me to go ahead.

I picked up a script from the pile on the table, not sure that I could do it. After all, I'd sounded like a New Yorker when I'd moved to Wyoming two years ago. But then I closed my eyes and imagined that I was with my friends Mary Jo and Mary Beth. How would they have read these lines? I opened my eyes and started to read. At the end of the speech I placed the script back on the table.

"That's how people really sound," I said.

Mr. Tidesdale beckoned to Mr. Peters, and the teacher walked over to him. There was some muttering with their heads together, then Mr. Tidesdale looked at me and said, "Can you sing?"

"Yeah, pretty well," I told him. "But I never took voice lessons or anything like that."

"Do you know any of the numbers from this show?" Mr. Tidesdale asked.

"I've heard them," I said. "They performed it at Cody High, for the Centennial of Buffalo Bill or something."

More laughter. Bailey was practically cackling. That only got me more determined than ever.

Mr. Peters handed me a music score and went over to the piano. "How about this one?" he asked. He started to play "You Can't Get a Man with a Gun."

I nodded. "I've heard it before."

"Well, then, go ahead. Sing it," he snapped.

I blinked back at him. "Me? You want me to sing it?"

"I'm not playing the piano for myself," he said.

Taking a deep breath, I started to sing. My throat felt dry, and my voice felt shaky. At first I sounded like a mouse squeaking in that big auditorium. But gradually I warmed up, and I stopped feeling scared. It was pretty obvious I was no Bailey, but this was definitely how the girl had sung it in Cody, which was about as authentic as you could get.

There was dead silence when I finished.

Nobody clapped. Feeling like a supreme idiot, I started to walk back to my seat. Mr. Tidesdale stood up and intercepted me.

"This is the girl that I want to play Annie," he said, placing a hand on my shoulder. "She's just how I pictured her. She's the real McCoy!" Then he shook my hand.

The rest of the afternoon passed in a blur. Auditions kind of fell apart after my whole performance. Mr. Tidesdale asked me a lot of questions about Indian Valley, and we compared breeds of cattle and roping techniques.

It was only when everyone was leaving the auditorium and Mr. Peters was congratulating me that I finally realized that this was really happening—I got the lead in the musical!

Suzanne rushed over to join me. "Miss Shy Girl, huh?" she demanded, her eyes laughing. "Am I talking to the person who didn't even think she was good enough to make the chorus?"

"I don't know how it happened," I told her, shaking my head. "I think I'm still in shock."

Bailey and two of her friends walked up to me. "I have to congratulate you," she said, glaring at me. I'm telling you, if looks could kill, I'd have dropped dead on the spot. "You sure planned that well, didn't you? Pretending you just wanted to correct our accents—and that lasso business—what a great way to get noticed! What are you going to do when we perform *Miss Saigon*—claim you're Vietnamese?"

"No," I stated. "I really did just move here from Wyoming. And you really did sound like Elly May."

"As if that matters," Bailey responded. "Hickstown is Hickstown to New Yorkers. Anyway, I'm glad you got the part. The role needs that kind of out-of-tune, flat, and scratchy voice. You'll be just great."

Then she and her friends pushed past me. I stood there frozen in place for a moment, feeling kind of sick and scared. But then I thought, *I got the part—she didn't,* and I started to smile.

I don't remember leaving the building that day. I sort of floated past all those other people who looked at me curiously or enviously. I was the only one who knew I'd definitely gotten a part since Mr. Tidesdale had handpicked me. Everyone else was going to have to wait until Monday to find out. Classmates kept coming up to me and saying, "Congratulations, Amber," and I kept on smiling like an idiot and saying, "Thank you."

I think Suzanne was as excited as I was. She talked nonstop all the way home—not that that was so unusual for her.

"This is going to be so cool, Amber," she said when we were in front of my apartment building. "Think of the cast parties. Think of how good it will look on your college applications! Boy, you really struck gold. I'm so happy for you . . . and I bet that Sean O'Brien will get the male lead. He is *so* gorgeous! And he's nice too."

I continued to float into my building and up-stairs in the elevator. Beau and Katie were sitting at

79

the kitchen table, already working on their homework, when I walked into our apartment.

"Guess what, guys?" I yelled to them. "I just got the lead in the musical!"

"Wow, Amber. You're going to be a star," Katie said.

"You were the best one in the whole school?" Beau asked.

"I know I wasn't the best," I said. "I lucked out. They're doing this play about the Wild West, and I was just right for the part. An old guy from Texas is putting up the money, and he liked the way I threw the lasso."

"That's it?" Beau demanded. "You got the part because you could throw a dumb rope?"

"Well, he liked the way I sang too," I added hastily. "I'm so excited. I'm going to go learn my lines."

It was only when I sat on my bed and opened the script that reality hit me—I had a ton of lines to memorize. I looked at the rehearsal schedule that Mr. Peters had handed to me. We had practice almost every evening until the middle of November. And I was already worried that I wouldn't be able to handle my homework. Plus what about that job I was going to get so that I'd have the money to fly to Wyoming?

"I can't do this," I said out loud, standing up. I'd just have to call Mr. Peters and tell him I'd made a mistake.

But then I thought about how Bailey would probably get the part instead—I could just imagine how smug she'd be. "I knew she couldn't hack it. She just wasn't good enough." I could hear her saying the words now.

I gritted my teeth. Somehow I was going to do this part, no matter how much time it took.

And what's more, I was going to do it well— brilliantly and better than Bailey!

I couldn't wait to tell Rich.

Eight

Rich

"HAVE YOU HEARD from Amber lately?" Mary Ann asked me. A group of cheerleaders had stopped me in the halls. It was all those Mary Somethings—Mary Jo and Mary Beth and Mary Ann, plus a couple of other girls.

"Yeah, she called me last night," I said. "We speak to each other most nights."

"Wow, that has to cost a lot," Mary Beth said.

I grinned. "But it's worth it. Letters take a couple of days, and I don't have e-mail. Besides, I really like being able to hear her voice."

"You're so sweet," Mary Jo said, nudging me.

"So, how's she doing?" asked Becky, the head cheerleader.

"Just great. She got the lead in the musical."

"That's wonderful! Well, she's so talented," Becky

said, smiling proudly as if she was Amber's mother. "Tell her we miss her, will you? Tell her we're using one of her routines for state championship this year."

"Why don't you tell her yourself? I know she'd love to hear from y'all."

"Okay, we'll write to her," Mary Beth said. "But still say hi from us when you talk to her again. Tell her congratulations. We're glad she's doing so well."

"Sure thing," I said, then smiled and walked on.

As I headed down the hall, I tried to tell myself that I was glad for Amber too. She'd sounded so excited when she called me Friday night—she was back to her old bubbly self.

"It's a huge commitment, Rich," she'd told me. "I'm worried I won't be able to handle it."

"You really want to do this, don't you?"

"Are you kidding? The lead in the school musical? Of course I want to! It's like a dream come true. Do you know how many important people come to watch our musicals—directors from Broadway, talent scouts, college professors? If I'm good, maybe some drama program will offer me a scholarship."

Amber's words echoed through my head all weekend. If a drama program offered her a scholarship, it sure as heck wouldn't be a school near Wyoming. It would be one of those colleges back east. And if she went to school at one of those places, I'd never see her again.

Suddenly I felt like I'd stepped into an empty elevator shaft and I was falling, falling, falling. . . . She was doing so well, she was so happy, and I didn't even have my starting slot back on the football team. What chance did I have of getting a scholarship now?

At football practice that afternoon I tried to give it everything I had, but my shoulder was still hurting from that horrible game, and it felt like my legs had lead weights in them. I seemed to have lost that bounce in my stride that had allowed me to dodge past defenders.

I was thinking about this as I pulled into my driveway that evening. I saw Sultan looking at me over the corral fence when I parked my truck. Just one more reminder of how I'd been failing lately.

Well, enough was enough.

"You no-good horse," I said, getting out of my truck. "It's about time someone whipped you into shape."

I ran inside the house, threw my schoolbooks onto the kitchen table, and went to get his saddle and bridle. I was going to get Sultan in shape no matter how much work it took.

He tried to dance around while I put the saddle on him. This time I gave him a good whack on his rump. He looked surprised long enough for me to get the saddle on correctly.

"You're going to learn how to behave," I told him as I swung myself up into the saddle. Then I started to take him around the corral. I could feel the power in his haunches—he was just itching to go. But I kept Sultan reined in and slowed him to a trot. He kept trying to shake his head loose, but I wasn't about to give an inch. Then he danced sideways, tucked in his head, and tried to circle on me. I stuck my heels in his sides. This was clearly a battle of wills here. I'd better be the one to win.

Finally I got him going around the ring at an even pace. *Okay,* I thought. *I've got him under control. At least I can tell Amber that I'm doing something right in my life.*

Amber. I came back to our phone conversation the other night. I hadn't known she was even thinking about studying drama! She'd certainly never told me. Did she have other secret dreams that she hadn't shared with me? Suddenly I had the horrible thought that maybe I'd never really known her. Maybe she was one person here in Wyoming and a totally different person now that she was back in New York. . . .

The reins went slack in my hands as my thoughts wandered. Sultan threw up his head, then his heels. I went sailing off his back and landed hard in the dirt. I was just scrambling to my feet when I looked up and saw that I wasn't alone.

My neighbor Melanie was leaning on the fence rail, watching me. There was a grin on her face.

"What are you doing here?" I demanded, humiliated. "Don't you have anything better to do than sneak up and spy on people?"

"I thought I'd come over and watch you take flying lessons," she teased, still grinning. "Next time flap your arms. You won't hit the ground so hard."

"Very funny," I said, dusting myself off. "Where's that stupid horse now?" I muttered half to myself, looking around. Sultan was standing on the far side of the corral. The look on his face indicated that he was ready to run if I made a move toward him.

"Stupid, useless horse," I growled. I picked up my hat from where it lay in the dirt, then flung it down again in frustration.

"If you don't mind my saying so, you're doing it all wrong," Melanie told me.

I glared at her. "What are you—Wyoming's answer to the *Horse Whisperer*?"

"No, but I do know quite a bit about horses." She climbed through the fence rails and into the ring. Melanie walked over to Sultan, who didn't budge, then swung herself onto his back. I didn't even see the command she gave him, but he moved forward in an effortless lope, crisscrossed the ring, slowed to a trot, turned on a dime, then raced full speed to the far fence.

I stood there dumbstruck, feeling like an idiot. When Melanie brought him back to me, there was still a smile on her face. "Great horse you've got here," she said. "Did you know he's already been rodeo trained?"

She swung herself down and patted Sultan's rump. He stepped a pace away, then stood looking at her, waiting for her to tell him what to do next.

"That's amazing," I told her, shaking my head. "How do you do that?"

"Practice, I guess. I've worked around horses all my life."

"But you just moved from Denver."

"Where my dad ran a riding academy," Melanie explained. "And before that we had our own ranch

86

in Colorado. We had a couple of bad drought years there—a really bad winter when we lost most of our herd, so we had to sell up and leave. That was really hard. I loved that place. I was born there."

"Well, at least you get to live on a ranch again now," I said.

"It's not the same." She sighed. "It can never be the same. I feel like I don't belong here. I know we're not intending to stay, and it makes me feel like I'm invisible."

I looked at her, seeing her as a person with ideas and emotions for the first time. "You want to come inside for a while?" I asked. "My mom makes the best lemonade."

She smiled again. "Sure. What about the horse?"

"He'll be okay."

"Well, I'll just loosen his girth," she said. "No sense in letting him be uncomfortable."

It took her about two seconds to take care of Sultan, who didn't protest once. Then she slipped through the fence after me and walked beside me to the house.

"He just lets you do anything," I commented, shaking my head again.

"Yeah, well, he's not scared of me," she said. "Horses are herd animals. They have to decide that you belong to their herd and that you're not a threat. He's seen you as a threat from day one."

"Huh." I realized she was probably right—I'd set out to break him the first moment I saw him.

"I'll help you if you'd like," she offered. "I think

he'd make a great little rodeo horse. He turns even better than my Trixie."

My ears pricked up. "You know about rodeos?" I asked, opening the screen door for her.

"Sure. I've been in the senior rodeo division for a couple of years now—barrel racing, roping. The prizes are great. You can make good money."

Now she had my full attention. Good money? Enough for a plane ticket to New York? Then I frowned. "I've always wanted to try rodeos, but when I really think about it, I don't think I'd ever be good enough," I said.

"Sure, you would," Melanie said. "You've got a fast horse there. All you need to do is learn how to handle him." She took the glass of lemonade I handed her and sat down at the kitchen table. "I'd be happy to help you. It would help take my mind off things."

"Do you miss Denver?" I asked her.

"Not exactly. A *person* who lives in Denver." She looked down at her glass and smiled sadly. "My boyfriend's back there. I'm finding this really hard. . . ." Her voice trailing off, she looked back up at me. "You said your girlfriend used to live in our house?"

I nodded.

"I guess you're going through the same thing, then."

"Yeah." I could hardly believe that I felt so comfortable with someone I barely knew, but I heard myself saying, "It's really screwing up my life, Melanie. I can't concentrate. I can't do anything right. I miss her so bad, it hurts."

"I know how you feel," she said. "I can't stop thinking about David."

"At least Denver is close enough to drive to. Amber's gone clear across the country . . . to a whole other life."

"Yeah, well, I thought we'd get to see each other more," Melanie said, an angry edge to her voice, "but it's not working out that way. Stupid football season. Next weekend's no good because they have an away game on Saturday. And the weekend after is no good because they've got a home game—David won't be able to spend time with me. When is it going to be good—that's what I keep asking myself."

We sat there silently for a moment, both staring down at our glasses of lemonade.

"My big worry is that he'll meet someone else," she blurted out suddenly.

I glanced up from my glass. "*My* big worry is that she'll like it there so much, she'll never want to come back here." I leaned back in my chair, stretching out my legs. "We sort of promised we'd go to the same college next year. But Amber's smart, and she does really well in school. I thought I'd get a football scholarship. Now it doesn't look like that's going to happen."

"It is pretty tough to get a scholarship," Melanie agreed. "There aren't many of them, and there are loads of talented players. David thinks he'll get a scholarship too, but I'm not so sure."

I let out a heavy sigh. "The thing is, though, I made all-conference first team last year as a junior.

Plus I've been the school MVP for the past two years."

Melanie's eyebrows lifted. "That sounds promising."

"Except for the fact that I'm not playing like an MVP so far this season. Coach benched me—I fumbled the winning touchdown."

Melanie nodded, wincing. "I saw it," she told me. "But don't be so hard on yourself. Pros do the same thing, and they're paid a zillion dollars a year."

"No, I shouldn't have fumbled," I insisted, shaking my head in frustration. "I just wasn't concentrating hard enough. I was thinking about Amber and remembering what it was like when she was on the sideline cheering for me. She's haunting everything I do."

Melanie toyed with the rim of her glass. "Well, if Amber matters that much to you, you know what you've got to do, don't you? You have to make sure you two end up at the same school."

I blinked back at her. She was the first person *not* to tell me that it was time to move on and say good-bye to Amber. "That's a nice thought," I said quietly. "But it's much easier said than done."

"It's up to you, Rich," she stated firmly. "Look, I'm not just lecturing you. I know what it's like. I broke my leg in a bad fall a couple of years ago. I was terrified to get back on my horse. I thought I'd never get back into good enough shape to win rodeos."

"So what did you do?"

"I forced myself to work twice as hard. I wouldn't let all my fears beat me. It took a while, but eventually I was back to my top form. So maybe you have to work twice as hard as usual on your football right now, but it'll pay off, trust me." She bit her lip, smiling. "Listen to me. I'm talking like I'm your mother or coach or something, and we only just met."

I smiled back at her. "Well, I'm glad for that," I said. "Nobody else seems to understand what I'm going through. The guys on the team, my coach, even my parents are telling me to forget about Amber. They think I should get over her and meet a new girl."

"What do they know about it?" Melanie demanded, her cheeks turning pink. "Maybe they've never really been in love. I know I'd never get over David in a million years. And if he started to get interested in another girl, I'd be down there like a shot and she'd have to fight me for him!"

She looked so funny, a tiny girl sitting there with this tough scowl on her face, that I burst out laughing. I think it was the first time I'd really laughed since Amber had left.

Melanie laughed too. "That's better," she said. "We've got to keep smiling."

"You're right," I agreed, my laughter dying down. I took a big gulp of my lemonade. "Hey, by the way, what did you come over for in the first place? You must have had a reason."

She shrugged. "I just wanted to say hi and see how the horse was getting along." She bit her lip again. "I don't know too many people yet. I guess I needed a friend."

"Well, I guess I needed one too," I said. "I'm glad you showed up when you did."

"Good." She stood up, placing her glass in the

sink. "So, would you like me to work with the new horse? I'd be more than happy to teach you what I know. I think he'd be great for events like calf roping."

"That's something I can do," I said, standing up as well. "I do it every year when I go with my dad to select the calves."

"We'll start working whenever you want, then," she said. "My dad's going to buy some mustangs at the next sale and break them, but until then we don't have much work around our place, so my time's pretty much my own."

"Great. That would be great."

She headed for the door. "Should we start tomorrow, about this time?"

"Okay."

"I'd better be getting back. I usually call David around six."

We went outside. The setting sun was making everything glow pink. Sultan was standing there, his coat glowing pink too.

"What about the horse?" she asked. "Are you going to work him more tonight?"

"Nah, I think I'll wait for the expert," I said. "No sense in starting off on the wrong foot with him. I'll get him unsaddled and watered."

"You need any help?" she asked cautiously. Obviously she didn't think I knew enough to unsaddle my own horse.

"I do know a bit about horses, you know," I said. "I've ridden all my life. It's just this son of a gun I'm having problems with. But he's going to have to learn to get used to me whether he likes it or not."

"Just stay out of the way of his feet," she said, grinning. "Bye, Rich. I'm really glad I came over."

"Me too. Bye, Melanie."

I walked her to the gate, and I smiled to myself as I walked back. I felt like the black cloud that had settled over me might be beginning to lift.

Nine

Amber

Dear Rich,

I'm writing this in history class, which is superboring. Do I really need to know how the legislature passes a bill? I'm not planning to run for Congress someday. Anyway, I'm writing because I'm thinking about you and wishing you were here and also because I feel really, really bad about last night.

I'm sorry I got home too late to call you. I just lost track of time. Rehearsal went on until six-thirty, and then a bunch of us went over to this girl Jill's house to study and grab some dinner—she lives right near school. Then we all went out for coffee. There's this coffee shop where we always hang out—Fiorelli's. I think I must have told you about it before—they make great homemade biscotti and excellent lattes. So we were all sitting there, talking about life, and when I looked at the time it was midnight—too late to call you, even with the time difference.

I hope you weren't sitting by the phone, worrying about me. I'm sure that's what I'd have been doing if you'd promised to call me and didn't. I'd be imagining all kinds of horrible things—that you'd crashed your truck or fallen off Sultan or something. I know I'll talk to you before you get this letter, but I just wanted to put it all down on paper now so you'll know how I'm feeling.

The play is going really well. I'm so glad I decided to do it. And I'm managing to get everything done—I'm learning how to survive on five hours' sleep. Of course, I can't survive too many evenings like last night. I still had some homework to do when I finally got home.

My big problem is that there just isn't enough time to do everything I want to. There's this international film festival this week and Dover students are volunteer ticket takers, which also means we get to see the movies for free. My theater-arts teacher has given us a list of movies he especially wants us to see—but there's also a free concert in Central Park, and I'd love to go to that too. And Beau has a soccer game, and I really should go cheer for him. Help!

Beau's fitting in almost too well. He beat up this bully on the first day, and now he's running with a really tough bunch of kids who think he's hot stuff. The latest is that he wants to get a tattoo. Mom and Dad are freaking, as you can imagine.

Katie's not doing as great. The kids think she's weird. They thought she was making it up when she said she had a pet lamb. She really misses her animals, and we can't have pets in our apartment. Mom bought her a turtle, but it's not the same. You can't hug a turtle, and it doesn't follow you around.

Whoops—the teacher is looking in my direction. I think he's going to call on me, and I don't know the answer. Bye.

Love,
Amber

P.S. He didn't. It was the guy behind me. *Phew*.

"Which movies do you want to sign up for?" Suzanne asked as we sat with our friends in the cafeteria later that day. "The Israeli film looks good, doesn't it? And the star, Lev somebody, is really, really cute. The stars sometimes show up at the performances, you know."

"It's on Friday night," I said, peering over at the

schedule she was holding. "I've got rehearsal until six."

"That's one of the big advantages of being in the chorus," Suzanne said. "Only two rehearsals a week until October."

"How's the play coming along?" Mandy asked.

"Okay, so far," Suzanne responded. "Although the Broadway choreographer guy they've hired takes it very, very seriously. If you do one arm movement different from how he's demonstrated it, he has minor hysterics. Luckily we only have three numbers we have to learn."

"Unlike *Amber,* who has billions and billions of numbers to learn," Thomas commented, throwing a piece of bagel in my direction.

I rolled my eyes. "Tell me about it. We have to have our lines and blocking down pat by three weeks from now. I know the first scene, and that's it. I never seem to have the time to memorize lines."

"I don't know how you guys manage to be in the play at all," Alicia said, pushing her salad around with a fork. "It takes me until midnight just to get my homework done."

"That's because you watch all of your favorite shows first," Mandy teased.

"Not all of them—just the good ones," Alicia said defensively. "And I haven't been able to watch a single episode of *Days of Our Lives* since school started."

We all started to laugh, and she smiled. "So?" she said. "I need my relaxation. I'm not willing to make sacrifices like Amber and Suzanne."

"Oh, yeah, sure, some sacrifice—playing opposite

Sean O'Brien," Suzanne said, giving me a knowing look. "Have you gotten into any of the love scenes yet, Amber? I'd put up with night after night of grueling rehearsals to get into a clinch with that guy."

I grinned—Suzanne always had guys on the mind. "Give me a break!" I said. "All we do is read lines and block out scenes. I've hardly said two words to him that aren't in the script."

"Well, if you want to say six more words, you could try, 'Cute friend. Wants date. Name's Suzanne,'" she suggested.

This time Thomas threw a piece of bagel at Suzanne.

Suzanne giggled. "It was just a suggestion."

"What's Sean like, Amber?" Mandy asked.

I shrugged. "He seems nice. We're always working so hard that we don't get much chance to talk. He takes the play very seriously." I paused, taking a sip of my apple juice. "But he's never made me feel like I'm not good enough for the show or that I should never have gotten the part, which is how some of the other cast members treat me."

"Like Bailey?" Mandy asked.

"No, Bailey quit, didn't you hear?" Suzanne told her.

"Bailey backed out of a musical? Is civilization as we know it coming to an end?" Thomas chuckled.

"She said the dumb musical wasn't worthy of her talents," I said, smiling at the happy memory. "Then she made a grand exit. She tried to get Sean to do the same, but he stayed."

"Interesting," Alicia commented. "That must mean it's all over between them."

My ears pricked up. "Sean and Bailey? They were together?" That was hard for me to believe. Sean seemed so nice and genuine. What could he see in Bailey . . . apart from the fact that she was gorgeous?

"Yeah, last year," Suzanne confirmed, nodding. "They were in all the same shows, so they hung out together. I don't know if it was ever serious, though."

God, I hope not, I thought. Then I stopped myself. What did *I* care whether Sean O'Brien liked Bailey or not? He was just some guy I was acting with.

"Someone as mean as Bailey shouldn't be allowed to go out with someone as cool as Sean," Mandy put in. "It's just not fair."

As I watched my girlfriends continue to go on about Sean—while Thomas rolled his eyes—I realized that every other girl at Dover would kill for a chance to be close to Sean. *Meanwhile,* I thought, *I get to spend all this time with him and I'm not even interested. The guy I want to be with is thousands of miles away.*

I sighed, getting up from the table. *I guess that's just how life is.*

Still, I couldn't help checking Sean out at rehearsal that afternoon. After all, my friends hadn't been able to stop gushing about him. I was only human.

I snuck a glance at him as I stepped into the theater. He was walking onto the stage. Definitely cute, that was for sure. His blond hair was long—straight and parted in the middle. And his blue eyes were very intense. I also liked how his hair flopped down across his forehead when he bent to put his books on a chair. In fact, if I hadn't been dating Rich, I might have been very interested indeed. Except that he did always seem so serious.

Sean was a total pro. He had his lines memorized, he never missed a cue, he took notes all over his script, and Mr. Peters never had to tell him anything twice.

I glanced around the auditorium and saw that we were the only ones there. "Hey, Sean. Where is everybody?" I asked.

"Oh, hi, Amber," he said, glancing up. "It's just you and me today. It's on the rehearsal schedule. We're going through our duets in act one."

"Oh, cool, I've got those memorized." I dropped down into a seat. "It's the lines in between I'm having trouble with."

"It helps to practice them out loud," Sean said, jumping off the stage and sitting down next to me. "I always tape the scenes I'm learning—except for my lines. Then I play it back and say my lines at the cues. I find that really helps."

I smiled at him, impressed. "That's a great idea. I've tried using my family to help me, but everyone's too busy except my little sister, and she can't read half the words."

"Yeah, well, no one's ever home at my house," Sean explained. "My parents are both theater people. They're gone for the night when I get home."

"Your parents are real actors?" I blurted out. My cheeks suddenly heated up—there I went, sounding like a backwoods hick again.

"Nothing so glamorous," Sean responded, grinning. "My mom's in wardrobe, and my dad's a lighting designer. But I suppose that's why I have theater in my blood. They always brought me backstage with them when I was a baby."

"Wow, how exciting!" I exclaimed, not caring whether I sounded like a hick or not. "I bet you've met lots of famous people."

"A few," he said. Then he glanced around. The room was still deserted. He cleared his throat. "Amber, I've got a favor to ask you."

I couldn't imagine what that could possibly be. He was the experienced one. "Yes?"

"Would you show me how to throw a rope? You know I have to lasso you in that scene, and I don't want to look like a jerk when we run through it today."

I laughed—he looked so nervous and cute, his eyebrows scrunched up in concern. "Sure, I can show you, no problem," I told him.

A smile broke out on his face. Whoa. He looked even cuter when he smiled like that. "Thanks," he said.

I hopped onto the stage and picked up the prop rope. "The thing is, this isn't the right kind of rope.

Real lassos are stiff, which makes it much easier to toss them. Maybe I'll ask my, um, friend in Wyoming to send me one."

Wait a minute, I thought, staring down at the rope. *Why did you hesitate there? Why didn't you say "boyfriend" instead of "friend"?*

I shook my head, telling myself to forget about it—it was just a slip of the tongue.

I made a good-sized loop with the rope. "Now, let's say I'm aiming for that chair," I said, motioning to a seat in front of me. "I hold the lasso in front of myself like this, I aim, and . . . voilà!" The rope landed neatly over the back of the chair.

"Cool," Sean said. "Would you do it again?"

"Sure." I demonstrated once more, then said, "Here, you try." I handed him the rope.

He stood up. "Well, it looks simple enough," he said. But he ended up throwing the entire rope instead of just the loop.

I giggled. "You forgot to hang on to one end," I told him. "It would be of no use if the cow ran away with the rope, would it?"

"I have to tell you, I'm clueless," he admitted. "I don't have great eye-hand coordination. In fact, I'm a klutz."

"You don't look like a klutz to me," I said playfully. Then I blushed. Had I sounded flirtatious? I didn't mean to flirt with Sean—at least I hadn't planned on it. . . .

Sean shook his head. "Trust me, I'm a clumsy fool. And if you can teach me how to throw a rope so that I

102

don't look like a total idiot, I'll love you forever."

I blinked back at him for a moment, caught off guard by his words. Then I reminded myself that he was just teasing and being dramatic. *After all,* I thought, *he's an actor. So chill out, Amber. Don't take him so seriously.*

We practiced lassoing some more, and Sean had almost gotten the hang of it by the time Mr. Peters and the music director showed up.

We performed our songs well that day. I was getting more confident in my singing, and everyone seemed to like the way I sounded. Plus the songs were fun to sing. Today we rehearsed the boasting duet, where I sang, "Anything you can do, I can do better."

"I want you to have fun with this," Mr. Peters told me. "Really ham it up."

I guess I got carried away. In one verse I was supposed to say, "Can you bake a pie? No, neither can I." Instead I sang, "When you throw a rope, you look like a dope."

That was it—Sean and I both cracked up. Had I thought that Sean was too serious? At that moment he proved me wrong, collapsing onto the nearest chair, tears streaming down his cheeks. Seeing him lose it like that made me laugh even harder—I had to lean against the wall for support.

Mr. Peters watched us patiently, a small smile on his face. "Now, if you can make the audience laugh like that, we're getting somewhere," he said, which started both of us off again.

We managed to get through the rest of the rehearsal without any more laugh attacks. We were just getting our stuff together to leave when the auditorium door opened and Bailey walked in.

"Oh, Sean, you're still here," she said, not even acknowledging my presence. "I thought I'd check in on you and see how it's going."

"It's going fine, Bailey," Sean said in a clipped voice. "Why are *you* here this late?"

"I was rehearsing for my senior recital. I'm doing all opera, I think. Someone has to show these morons what good singing sounds like." I gritted my teeth—clearly that comment was directed at me. "Anyway, are you done?" she asked Sean. "I thought we'd go have coffee."

"Sorry, but Amber and I already have plans," Sean responded quickly.

I froze in place, surprised, as Bailey shot me one of her lethal looks. "You and Amber?" she asked as if she were saying, *"You and a cockroach?"*

"That's right," he said. "See ya, Bailey. Ready, Amber?" He turned to look at me, a pleading expression on his face.

"Um, sure," I said, grabbing my book bag and following him out the door.

As soon as we were out of Bailey's earshot, he squeezed my arm. "Thanks for playing along."

"You didn't want to go have coffee with Bailey?" I asked, confused.

He wrinkled his nose. "I can't stand the girl. She drives me crazy."

"But I thought that you and she——"

"So did she," he interrupted, nodding. "She spread that rumor around the school, but I never asked her out, I swear. I do have good taste in most things." He smiled, and I smiled back at him. He really had a very cute smile. Plus I was happy to find out that he didn't like Bailey either. Not that it should have mattered or anything.

"So, would you like to go for coffee anyway?" he asked. "We could go over lines together."

"Okay," I said. "But let's make sure it's not the same place Bailey's going to."

He grinned. "Trust me, I'll make sure of that."

We ended up going to a Greek café that served sticky baklava and very strong coffee, where we sat and talked for hours. I told him about Wyoming, and he told me all about Broadway. Sean had a lot of great stories. I could have sat there all night, just listening to him.

"I guess I should get home," I said when I glanced outside and noticed that it was dark. "My parents will wonder where I am. And I have a ton of homework."

"Yeah, me too," he said. "I'm thinking of giving up sleep. It's a waste of time." He stood up. "Where do you live? I'll walk you home."

"That's okay. It's not far."

"It's New York, and it's dark. I'll walk you home," he insisted.

It was only when I was alone, riding the elevator up to my apartment, that I realized I hadn't told

Sean about Rich. He just hadn't come up in conversation for some reason.

Rich! I glanced at my watch, sprinting to the phone the moment I got inside the door. Thank God it wasn't too late to call him—there's no way I could miss him two nights in a row.

"Rich, honey, I'm sorry," I said when I heard his voice. "I'm sorry that I didn't call you yesterday."

"I figured you must be kind of busy these days," he told me.

"Kind of busy is an understatement." I plopped down onto my bed. "We have rehearsal after school every day. And since I'm in almost every scene, I always have to be there."

"So, how's it going?"

"Great. I really think I'm right for the part. You know I don't have a wonderful voice or anything, but I sound right for some reason. And it's fun too. I went out for coffee with Suzanne and my friends from the chorus last night, and we all sat there, just talking and laughing for hours."

"And tonight?" he asked.

"Same thing," I said. "Went out for coffee after rehearsal. There's this—" I was going to tell him about Sean and how nice he was and how easy he was to talk to, but I suddenly shut up. Would Rich really want to hear about that?

"This what?" he asked.

"This, um, tradition at Dover. We always study lines in the coffee shop. It's a good way to learn lines together."

Okay, so that wasn't a total lie. We *had* gone through our lines together. And I would tell him about Sean soon. As soon as I could be certain that Rich would understand. The last thing I wanted was for him to be jealous.

"Sounds like fun. When is this play anyway?"

"The middle of November, right before Thanksgiving," I told him.

"Well, I might just come and see it."

My heart leaped—I couldn't believe what I was hearing. "Are you serious? You'd come all the way to New York to see my play?"

"I might."

I bounced up and down on my bed with excitement. "Rich—that would be incredible!" Then I stopped bouncing. Reality hit. "Do you think you could afford it?"

"There's a good shot I'll have some money by then," he said mysteriously.

"How come? Did you get a job? Rich Winters—did you get a job and not tell me?"

"Not yet, but I've got some ideas. And if they pan out well, then I'll definitely have the money to fly to New York."

"And you're not going to tell me what those ideas are?"

"Not yet. Not until I'm kind of sure."

"Rich—that's so mean!" But I was laughing, bubbling over with happiness at the thought of seeing Rich again in November. I sighed. "So life's going better for you now?" I asked him.

"Much better. I'm keeping myself really busy, just like you are, and I'm working my butt off at football. That way I don't have so much time to just sit around and miss you."

"I know—it's the same way for me. I guess hard work is a cure for most things, isn't it?"

"You betcha." He laughed. It was good to hear him laugh. I missed that laugh more than anything. "So hang in there, babe. It won't be long before I'm out there to take New York City by storm."

I was still smiling ear to ear when I hung up. It was so great to hear his voice, to hear his laugh, and to feel that he was still close to me. That we were still close to each other.

I lay back on my bed and closed my eyes, imagining what it would be like when Rich came to visit. Maybe we'd do all the corny stuff, like take a carriage ride through Central Park and kiss on the top floor of the Empire State Building.

The sudden ringing of the phone jarred me back to the present. I hoped it wasn't Suzanne. I had too much homework piled up to talk right now. But my pulse raced at the thought that maybe it was Rich, calling me back with something he'd forgotten to say. He'd done that before in the past, even when he'd simply forgotten to say, "I love you."

"Hello?" I said, picking up the receiver.

"Amber, it's Sean."

That threw me for a curve. How did he know my phone number? "Oh, hi, Sean. What's up?"

"I just wanted to tell you that I had a great time tonight. You're so easy to talk to."

"I had a good time too. I loved hearing all your stories."

"Amber, I was wondering—" He paused for a long moment, and I wondered where he was going with all this. "You know the film festival this weekend? One of the theaters is having an old-movie marathon on Saturday night. Would you like to go with me? Maybe we could get a bite to eat afterward. . . ."

I cringed. This was sounding suspiciously like a date. "It sounds like a lot of fun, Sean—"

"Awesome. I'll pick you up about seven, then?"

I took a deep breath. Rich's warm voice was still echoing through my head. "Okay. But I should tell you something first. I have a boyfriend, back in Wyoming. I don't know why I didn't mention him sooner. Anyway, I'd love to hang out with you, but just as friends, okay?"

"All right," he said. There was an awkward pause, then he said, "Friends is just fine. They always say not to get involved with your leading lady, don't they?" He laughed, sounding nervous. "So I'll see you tomorrow at school, then. And I'm really looking forward to Saturday."

"Me too," I said, my heart pounding, then hung up the phone.

You did it, I told myself, closing my eyes and lying back in bed. *You told him you have a boyfriend. Now you have nothing to feel guilty about . . . do you?*

Ten

Rich

"WOWWEE! ALL RIGHT! Way to go, Rich!" Melanie yelled, waving her hat in the air. "You've got it now."

"Sultan's got it, you mean," I said shyly. Still, I was flattered that Melanie thought I was doing better with roping.

She walked over and patted Sultan's steaming flank. "He knows what's expected of him. You're finally working as a team."

"About time, huh?" I asked, grinning down at her.

She nodded. "It's taken a little while."

"You've been very patient with me, Melanie. I really appreciate all the time you've put into this."

She shrugged. "It's not like I have a load of other stuff to do." Her eyes smiled as she looked over at me. "I'm really excited for you, Rich. And now it's time for you to do it for real, at the rodeo next month."

"I was thinking about entering," I admitted. "You think I'll be ready?"

"You'll never know unless you try. You could enter the calf roping—what have you got to lose?"

"My dignity," I said. "I'd hate to look like a fool."

"You won't," she assured me. "That's one good horse you've got yourself there. Trust him. And if you do well, you'll come home with a few hundred dollars in your pocket."

I felt a big grin spread across my face. "My plane ticket to New York, you mean." I could hardly contain my excitement. "I could keep it a surprise, Melanie! I won't tell Amber for sure whether or not I'm coming, and then I'll just show up at her school—with roses! Can you imagine how shocked she'll be?"

"She's a lucky girl," Melanie said, kicking her boot toe into the soft dirt. "I wish David cared that much about me."

I placed my hand on her shoulder. "I'm sure he does."

"Yeah, right. He cares so much that he forgets to call and then tells me that he doesn't have any time for me."

"It's probably just that football keeps him so busy. Especially if he has a demanding coach. Maybe he'd love to get away, but he can't risk upsetting his coach."

She looked back up at me. "But I could still go there, couldn't I? Even if he's got games and work-outs, he'd at least have time to go for a soda with me!"

I squeezed her arm. "You could do what I was just talking about with Amber! Don't tell him you're coming, and then just show up at one of his games."

Her eyes widened, a smile breaking out across her face. "I could, couldn't I? The question is, do I dare?"

"Why not?"

"He might get mad at me."

I raised an eyebrow. "He'd get mad at his girl-friend for coming to watch him play?"

She laughed, shaking her head. "I guess not. I guess he'd be pretty psyched to see me." She paused for a moment, patting Sultan some more. "You know Rich, I think I'm going to do it. I'll call his parents and let them in on the secret. Then they can tell me which weekend would be good."

"That sounds perfect," I told her.

"Wow, this is going to be great!" She slapped her hand against her side, making Sultan dance sideways. "I'm really glad I met you, Rich Winters. You're a lifesaver. Do you think Amber would mind if I gave you a big hug?"

She didn't wait for an answer but flung her arms around my neck in one grand movement.

"Just remember, you better not make that trip three weeks from now," I told Melanie, pulling away from her. "That's homecoming weekend."

"Why do I need to be here for homecoming?"

she asked. "I'm not going to be the queen. I'm not even going to the dance."

I could hear the sadness in her voice, and I realized that she probably *would* have been the queen at her old school. "Tell you what," I said. "I wasn't planning on going to the dance either, on account of Amber not being here. But do you want to go with me? I mean, it's our senior year—we shouldn't miss it."

Melanie's face lit up. "Rich, I'd love to."

"Great. We'll be two horse-training buddies, keeping each other company while our loved ones are far away."

The smile faded from her face. "Are you sure it would be okay with Amber?"

I scratched my head—I couldn't say that I was. "Are you sure it would be okay with David?" I asked.

"No. Maybe I just won't tell him." She laughed. "I mean, I bet he doesn't tell me what goes on at those parties with all the cheerleaders."

I nodded. "You know and I know that we're just friends, but they might get the wrong idea."

Melanie giggled. "Now I'll have to come to the game and watch you score touchdowns."

"I hope I do. I think I'm playing better again. At least Coach has given me my starting slot back."

Sultan got tired of standing still and started to jerk his head around.

"Well, do you want to try what we've practiced a few more times?" Melanie asked. "You should make sure that it sticks in his head."

"Good idea," I said. "Now that I know I've got to be good enough to enter a rodeo, I'd better start working extra hard."

It was quite dark by the time I'd rubbed down Sultan and given him his evening mash. The whole time I was out there with him I was listening for the phone, anxiously waiting for Amber to call.

We'd agreed that it made more sense for Amber to call me since it was later in New York and she never knew what time she'd get home from rehearsal. That director sure worked her hard. Some nights she wasn't even home before I went to bed. But at least she sounded happy . . . too happy, sometimes.

I knew I was being a grouch and not fair to her, but it bugged me that her life was suddenly so full. She had film festivals and concerts and who knew what else to keep her occupied when she wasn't rehearsing—all the things she hadn't had out here in Wyoming. Did she even miss me at all? I wondered. Would she even be glad to see me if I surprised her in New York?

"Get a grip on yourself, Winters," I said out loud. Sultan looked at me like I'd gone off my rocker. *You know Amber's missing you as much as you're missing her,* I thought. *She's just doing all this stuff to keep herself busy. And if she's having a good time while she does it, that's great.*

I gave Sultan a slap on his rear and crossed the yard to the house. Once I got settled inside, I tried to work on a science report. But I ended up just

114

reading the same page in my textbook over and over again. The words wouldn't stick in my brain— I had too many distracting thoughts that interfered.

Is Amber going to get home too late to call me again? I wondered miserably. How could any dumb old rehearsal take that long? And if she was out at that coffee place again, how come she was having such a good time that she forgot to call me?

I chewed on my pencil. I went to make myself a snack. I paced around my room. Finally, just before ten o'clock, she called.

"Sorry, Rich," she gasped, as if she'd been running. "I know it's late. I hope I haven't woken your parents."

"It's okay. I got the phone on the first ring. You sound out of breath."

"I am." She laughed. "I got to my building, and the elevator wasn't working. So I had to walk up twelve flights of stairs. I'm not in Wyoming shape anymore, Rich. I was huffing and puffing the whole way up."

"I don't like the thought of you walking up those stairs by yourself," I said. "Aren't stairwells dangerous places in New York?"

"Oh, don't worry. I wasn't alone," she told me. "This—another person from the play was with me. We're going through our lines together. So, what's up with you? Can you tell me any more about the mysterious job yet? Did you get it?"

"It's not exactly a job," I said. "And I'm not sure that I've got it, but it's possible."

115

"Rich, you're being so annoying!" She giggled. "If I was there, I'd grab you and tickle you until you told me."

I laughed. "I bet you would. You're a demon tickler."

"Only because you have to be the most ticklish guy in the world. Give me a hint—is it a job I wouldn't expect you to get? Are you working at a beauty parlor or a day-care center or something?"

"Not even close!" I grinned to myself and shook my head. God, I missed her! "Okay, if you really want to know—I'm training to enter the rodeo circuit."

"Rodeos?"

"You don't sound too thrilled."

"Rich, you know how I feel about rodeos. I don't want you getting trampled by a horse or gored by a bull."

I sat down on my bed. "I'm not going to do that kind of stuff," I told her. "Just calf roping. They have very strict rules so that the riders don't get hurt, so don't worry. Okay?"

She let out a sigh. "I'll try not to."

"The prize money is great, Amber. It'll sure help pay for a lot of plane tickets. . . ."

"*If* you win."

"I think I have a good shot. We've been working with Sultan—he's a natural for rodeos. He can turn on a dime, and he's got the quickest reactions you've ever seen."

"So he's stopped trying to throw you?"

"Oh, yeah. We get along great now. Melanie

116

told me that horses have to accept you as a member of their herd before they'll work well with you." I laughed. "I guess I'm now an official herd member."

"Melanie?" Amber asked. "The girl who moved into my house?"

"Yeah. Didn't I tell you that she was helping with Sultan?"

"No," Amber responded.

"Oh, wow, I guess we really haven't been able to talk a lot. Anyway, Melanie's been in the senior rodeo division for a couple of years now. She's teaching me everything she knows."

"Everything she knows, huh?"

I could hear tension in Amber's voice. "Hey, what's wrong?" I asked her.

"Nothing. Why should there be? I'm just thrilled to hear that some girl is teaching you everything she knows."

I sighed. "About *horses,* Amber. What's the matter—don't you want me to be able to make the money to come and see you?"

"As long as you don't bring Melanie along with you," she said in a teasing voice. I couldn't tell if she was still mad or not.

"Don't be silly," I told her. "You've got nothing to be jealous about. Hey, if I was going to take up with another girl, you don't think I'd choose the one who moved into your old house, do you? That would be a little close for comfort." I hoped my joke would lighten the mood of our conversation.

"If she was pretty enough," Amber said. "You told me she was cute."

"Well . . . she is. But I'm not interested, so quit worrying." Amber didn't respond, so I changed the subject quickly. "Anyway, tell me. What have you heard from your grandpa?"

"Not much. I think my dad called him last Sunday, but I was out. I've been meaning to write— I just never seem to have time. I hope he'll come and have Thanksgiving in New York with us."

"I think I'll give him a call," I said. "I miss the old guy. In spite of what you seem to think, I don't like the idea of new people in his house. I wish the winter would hurry up and be over so that he could come home."

"I wish the same thing, Rich. I wish this year would hurry up and be over so that we could be together again."

"Me too, babe. I'm trying my best at everything—I'm working like crazy on my football so that I can get into a good school and be with you."

"How do you have time for all this rodeo stuff if you're so busy with football?"

"I make time. Melanie comes over after dinner, and we work at it until it gets too dark to see. It's really nice of her to give up so much of her time, but she's like you. She needs something to keep her busy in a new place where she doesn't know too many people. It's hard trying to fit in as a senior. You should know that. That's why I'm . . ."

"You're what?"

"I'm looking out for her," I said quickly. I'd been about to blab that I was taking Melanie to the homecoming dance. *That* would have been a big mistake. Amber was obviously jealous of Melanie, even though she had no cause to be.

Nope, there was no reason to tell Amber that I was going to the dance with Melanie. What she didn't know wouldn't hurt her.

Eleven

Amber

"AMBER, WAKE UP!" Sean whispered in my ear.

I jumped. "What?" I had been miles away—about two thousand miles away to be exact.

"Don't miss your cue," Sean said, pushing me out onto the stage. My mind was a blur. Where were we? What scene were we on?

"Gee, Annie Oakley. I didn't expect to see you here," one of the chorus girls said, putting her hands on her hips. It was my cue! I was supposed to say something. I opened my mouth, hoping that my subconscious knew what I should say, but nothing came out.

"Sorry," I muttered, looking down at the ground. "Sorry, Mr. Peters. I just went blank."

"That's the second time today, Amber," he said.

"And you're supposed to be word perfect for acts one and two."

"I know, and I really do have the lines memorized. It's just that, well, I guess I'm overtired." I didn't think the fact that I was preoccupied with thoughts of Rich would cut it with Mr. Peters. "I have so much homework to do, and I never get to bed until late."

"It's the same for everyone else," Mr. Peters told me sternly. "You haven't been focused these past few days. Make sure you go through those lines this weekend—until you can say them in your sleep, okay?"

"Okay. I'm sorry. I'll try harder," I said, then walked back to the side where I was to make my entrance from.

Somehow I managed to get through the rest of rehearsal by making a superhuman effort of concentration. After it was over, I flopped onto the nearest chair. Sean came over and put a hand on my shoulder.

"What's up?" he asked.

"Just tired, like I said."

He shook his head. "No, it's more than that. You know those lines. We went through them together last week—you knew them perfectly."

"You're right," I said. "I've got things on my mind."

"Would it help to talk? I'm a good listener. . . ."

I hesitated. How could I tell a guy who liked me about my problems with my boyfriend? And I didn't know if I could talk to anybody about my problems with Rich. I certainly hadn't told Suzanne or my parents. I knew what they'd say—forget about him, it's over, move on. Suzanne had already told me that I needed my head examined for telling Sean O'Brien that I just wanted to be friends.

"We could go for a walk or some coffee or get something to eat," he added.

I looked at him, and he gave me a cute smile. I guessed it was worth a try—I needed to talk to someone or I'd burst. "Okay," I said. "Thanks."

"Walk first or eat first?" he asked.

"Eat first. I'm starving."

He laughed. "That's a good sign. It can't be too serious if you're still interested in food." He stood up. "Do you feel like Chinese? There's this little place that has great hot-and-sour soup. Cheap but filling."

"Sounds good to me," I said. "Especially the cheap part."

"Hey, it's my treat."

"No, it's not. If you're going to play therapist, the least I can do is pay for the food." I stood up as well. "I insist, Sean."

He put his hands up in surrender. "I never say no to a free meal."

It was a long walk, and a brisk fall wind blew off the East River, but it felt good to be out in the fresh air. It made me think of how I now spent most of my life in airless rooms. In Wyoming, I'd been out in the open air every day—riding or helping with

122

the cattle or going for a walk with Rich beside our little stream. . . .

A big sigh shook my body. Sean turned to me. "What's the problem?" he asked. "Boyfriend trouble?"

I nodded. I'd told him some more about Rich over the past couple of days, so he knew the major details. "He's met this new girl," I began. "Actually, she moved into our old house. Isn't that poetic?"

"And he wants to break up?"

"No, he says there's nothing between them, that they're just friends. But they're spending every moment together, Sean. She's helping him with his new horse, and he talks about her all the time. I know I shouldn't be jealous, but I just don't want him to admire another girl like that."

"You want him to have a life, don't you?"

"Yeah . . . but—"

"You just don't want him to enjoy it," Sean finished for me. I had to smile. "Right," I said as we stopped, waiting for the light to change.

"Well, you can't expect him to stay shut in his room all year just because you're not there," Sean said. "After all, you're out with me right now. What does he think about that?"

The light turned green, and we crossed the street. "I, um, haven't told him about you."

"Why not?"

"I thought he might get the wrong idea. I didn't want him to get jealous."

"Just like he's making you jealous because he's

working on a project with another girl?"

"Ugh, how come you guys always stick to-gether?" I demanded, navigating my way around a group of children. "Okay, so maybe I am overreacting, but he's spending every second with this girl. He's going to a rodeo with her all the way in Billings, Montana. I've called his house a couple of times this week and his mom says he's not home—at ten o'clock at night! That has to mean he's with Melanie, right?"

"I don't know," Sean told me as we reached the Chinese restaurant. "Maybe. Maybe not."

I sighed again as we walked inside. The place was tiny—a little hole-in-the-wall without much charm. But they served us right away with big bowls of steaming hot-and-sour soup. The warmth immediately took away the chill of the night wind.

Sean also ordered an appetizer tray, and we both laughed at our attempts to pick up prawn balls and wontons with chopsticks.

"You know what I think, Amber?" Sean said after we broke open our fortune cookies at the end of the meal. "I think that maybe you and Rich are getting over each other and it's time to move on."

I looked up to meet his eyes. "Don't say that. Rich and I are never going to get over each other." I shook my head. "I don't want him to like Melanie better than me, Sean. I couldn't bear it if he found another girl. This is tearing me apart."

Sean didn't say anything; he just played with his fortune cookie, breaking it into little pieces. "Then

124

I guess this fortune is wrong," he finally said, handing me the little strip of paper.

You will get your heart's desire, it said.

I looked into Sean's eyes. He was staring at me with such intensity. "Amber . . . ," he murmured.

My pulse quickened, but I tried to make light of the situation. "Mine says that I'm going to take a long trip in the next month, which shows you how wrong they are. I'm stuck here at least until Christmas."

Sean just nodded and smiled.

Phew, I thought, fiddling with my fortune, *what just happened there?* Sean obviously still liked me. But I had felt something too. Did I *want* something to happen? I had to admit that part of me sort of did.

I paid the bill, and we walked out of the restaurant. The brisk wind now cut into us like a knife. We huddled close together and walked quickly.

"I'm freezing," I said, my teeth chattering. "If I'd known it was going to turn into winter today, I'd have worn my big jacket."

"Here, I'll keep you warm," Sean said, slipping his arm around my shoulders and holding me close to him.

I wished he hadn't done that. His warmth and closeness were unnerving. Part of me wanted to push him away, but part of me didn't. I let him keep his arm around me.

We crossed Rockefeller Plaza. The spray from the fountain stung our faces.

"Hey, I know I probably need a cold shower, but no thanks," Sean yelled.

I laughed despite myself. Sean took my hand and dragged me out of the wind and spray. The plaza was deserted, and the lights from the building windows reflected in the wet pavement. The only sounds were the muted roar of traffic and the gentle splashing of the fountain. Sean was still holding my hand. And for some reason, I didn't want to let go.

"Yuck, now I'm wet *and* cold," I said, my brain reeling. What did I want to happen here? I didn't know. I just knew that it felt nice to be close to him. "My cheeks are stinging."

Sean put his hand up to touch my cheek. "Wow, you're icy," he said. His hand lingered on my cheek. "I should do something about that," he murmured, and before I really knew what was happening, he was kissing me.

My first reaction was surprise. *Stop this right now! It's crazy! Push him away,* my brain was screaming, but I realized that I didn't want him to stop. His lips were warm and firm against mine. Somehow my arms had slid around his neck and I was kissing him back.

"Amber," he whispered when we broke apart. "This is so right. You must know it's right. Don't you see—you've gone back to the person you really are. You're a city girl. You love theater and culture. And you belong with someone who loves those things too."

Oh God, what had I done? I could feel tears stinging my eyes. "Would you please take me home

126

now?" I asked quietly. "I need to go home. Somehow I have to make sense of all this."

"Okay. I understand." He took my hand, and we walked most of the way in silence.

"Amber," he said as we approached my building, "there's a teen night at a club in the Village tomorrow. A group of us are going. Would you like to come with me?"

This was happening too fast! "I'll call you in the morning," I told him. "I need to do some serious thinking first. And I have to talk to Rich. It wouldn't be fair to—" I broke off, tears catching in my throat. Then I shook my head and broke away from Sean, pushing my way through the revolving front door.

Once I was upstairs and safely shut in my room, I stood at the window and stared down at the lights across the park.

Was Sean right? Was I back where I belonged? Was Rich a part of my life that I'd left behind and could never go back to? I hadn't expected to like it when Sean kissed me, but I did. I'd even kissed him back.

My stomach turned over at the thought. Did that mean I was over Rich?

I walked across the room and picked up Rich's photo from my bedside table. That familiar wicked grin and that light brown hair sticking out from under his cowboy hat tore my heart in two. I didn't want to be over Rich. I didn't want him to belong to a part of my life that was in the past.

But was it realistic to think that we could keep up this long-distance relationship? It seemed like he was already meeting new girls and moving on. And what about me? I had just kissed another guy!

I glanced at the alarm clock. It was past eleven in Wyoming. Was it too late to call? I had to talk to him tonight. If he told me that everything was all right and that he loved me, then nothing else mattered. I'd call Sean in the morning and tell him I'd made a mistake.

There was a tap on my door.

"Amber—don't you want your letter?" Katie called. "You got a letter from Indian Valley."

I sprinted to the door and flung it open. Rich had written to me! This had to be a sign—everything was going to be okay. I snatched the letter from Katie's outstretched hand, but when I looked at it, I just said, "Oh."

The letter wasn't in Rich's handwriting. "It's from Mary Jo," I said flatly.

"Ask her how Lammie's doing when you write back," Katie said, walking away.

Sighing, I opened the envelope and curled up among my pillows to read it.

> Hi, Amber.
>
> How are you? We're all missing you here. The cheerleading squad isn't the same without you. We're going to enter the state champs in the spring, but I don't think we have much hope of placing this time.
>
> Rich told us that you got a big part in the play at your school. Congratulations!

We're all so proud of you. We know you'll be just great. Rich is doing okay—we keep an eye on him for you. He's working hard at his trick riding with that new girl who moved into your house. She's quiet and shy and keeps to herself a lot. She hasn't made too many friends, which must be why Rich is taking her to the homecoming dance—"

I dropped the paper as if it was on fire. He was taking Melanie to the homecoming dance! He *had* moved on—he'd already found someone else!

And then I thought about how I'd kissed Sean. Clearly I had moved on as well—there was no way this was going to work between us any longer.

I could hardly see the numbers on the phone through my tears as I dialed. I took a deep breath to compose myself as I heard his voice on the other end of the line. "Rich, it's Amber. We have to talk," I said.

"Hey, there, what's up?"

"I think you know as well as I do." I felt strangely calm now. Totally in control. "I think we both know it's over, don't we?"

"*What?* What are you talking about?"

"Rich—you're taking another girl to the home-coming dance. Doesn't that give me a little clue? You've found someone else, and I . . . I kissed another guy tonight, Rich."

"*You what?*" I thought the phone might explode in my ear from Rich's screaming. "You've

129

been dating someone behind my back?"

"Like you haven't?" Now I was yelling too. "Taking someone to the dance isn't dating? That's news to me. And all those times I've called and your mom doesn't know where you are. Give me a break, Rich. I'm not totally stupid."

"Fine," he snapped. "Fine, if that's how you want it. Boy, it sure didn't take you long to get over me."

"Just about as long as you took to get over me."

"Okay, if this is how you want to be, that's just great. Now I won't have to feel guilty about taking Melanie to the dance." He sounded so angry that he didn't even sound like himself. "Bye, Amber. Have fun with your new guy. Have a nice life, I guess."

Then the line went dead. I just stood there, holding the phone in my hand, staring at it.

What had I done? Rich's words, *Have a nice life,* played over and over again in my head.

I let out a sob. I had just lost Rich forever.

Twelve

Rich

I STOOD THERE, frozen, staring at the phone I had just slammed down. I was in total shock. Amber had found a new guy. She had kissed him. I felt like a knife was twisting in my gut as I imagined her with him. I squeezed my eyes shut, trying to make the image go away.

Why hadn't I suspected it before? All those nights when she'd gotten home so late from her rehearsals that she hadn't called me? What a fool I'd been. A total idiot. She hadn't been rehearsing until midnight. She'd been out with some jerk!

I had to stop myself from punching the wall. Instead I slammed my fist into the palm of my other hand. That was what I'd like to do to that guy— knock him down with one punch. Then I'd sweep Amber up and gallop away with her on Sultan's back.

But what if she didn't want to come with me? What if she was happy back in her old life and she liked this guy better than me? I paced around the kitchen in circles. What idiot had told Amber that I'd asked Melanie to homecoming anyway? What exactly had that person said to make Amber get the wrong idea? I'd been dumb not to tell her myself. She would have understood if I'd explained how lonely Melanie was and how we were just going as friends because I didn't want to miss out on my last homecoming.

But now it was too late. She'd found another guy, and it was all over. I couldn't believe I'd never see her again. I swallowed hard to stop the tears from coming to my eyes.

I didn't sleep at all that night. I lay in my cold, empty room, praying for sleep to come, but it wouldn't. Every time I closed my eyes, I'd see Amber's face. I'd see her gracefully running ahead of me along the creek-side trail, or in her bathing suit at the swimming hole, or smiling up at me when I held her in my arms—it was too painful to bear, so I decided I wouldn't close my eyes again all night.

Dumb idea, of course, because I'd completely forgotten about the big football game the next day. I went to school feeling like a zombie. My eyes prickled and burned. My tongue felt like a dried piece of toast. My limbs didn't seem to want to obey me.

Some wide receiver I'll be, I thought miserably as I changed in the locker room that afternoon.

All the other guys were talking excitedly, yelling at each other to get psyched up.

"Jefferson thinks they're so hot just because they've got Wiley Parks as quarterback," Chuck shouted. "You know what? He's not going to get to use that arm because I'm going to nail him first."

"And Winters is going to outrun that hotshot cornerback of theirs, right, Richie?" Wayne said, slapping me on the back.

"What? Oh, yeah, sure," I responded mechanically.

"What's with you, man?" Mike Morris demanded. "It's like you're on another planet again. This is a big game. Don't blow it for us."

"I'll try," I said. "I just can't seem to get revved up."

"Snap out of it, Rich." He leaned in closer to me. "Listen, I heard a rumor that the scout from Colorado State might be coming today. Think about it, Rich. Colorado State. Your whole future's on the line here."

Colorado State. It was one of the schools that Amber and I had discussed. It fitted what we both wanted, and it was a great school.

Just my luck, I thought. *The day the Colorado scout shows up, I'm like a walking zombie. I'm sure going to look impressive out there. I'll probably fall over my own feet.*

As we walked out onto the field, Chuck fell into step beside me. "Listen, Rich," he said. "There are a lot of guys counting on this game today. You're not the only one who'd like to look good for this scout. So don't blow it, okay? Remember, we're your teammates."

Then he pushed past me and jogged onto the field.

He's right, I thought, feeling a hot flush come to my cheeks. *I've been so wrapped up in myself that I haven't been thinking about anyone else. If I look bad out there, it makes the whole team look bad.* I made a mental vow to give it all I had, even if I did feel like curling up in a ball and crying.

The game kicked off, and I wasn't doing too well. I slipped and missed a step on my first run. I couldn't get free, and the quarterback had to throw to the tight end instead of me. Then the first time he threw to me, I almost dropped the ball. *Great,* I thought. *The scout has probably crossed me off his list already.*

We had to punt away, and I sat on the bench, feeling like the black cloud hanging over my head was getting bigger all the time. How could I let Amber mess up my life? My teammates had all been right—she was just a girl, that was all. And a guy was supposed to date a whole lot of girls before he settled down. Half the girls in the senior class would jump at a date with me. Amber had moved on. She was doing great—the lead in the play, a new guy. Okay, I decided, I was going to move on too. I'd show her that I wasn't missing her at all. Not one bit.

The Jefferson running back fumbled, and we were back on the field. I suddenly felt pumped and ready to go. It was like I'd turned to steel or something—no feelings, no emotions, just raw determination.

And I was a running and catching machine. The quarterback called the play. I had to go deep down the left side. I took off, feeling my legs pumping over that turf. The ball hung over me, then dropped neatly into my hands. Now the end zone was ahead of me, maybe by thirty yards. I kept on running. Soon I felt someone hit me from behind. Someone grabbed at my waist. Someone else was trying to hold on to my leg. But I just kept on going. The cornerback was ahead of me. I just went right through him like he wasn't there.

"I don't need you, Amber Stevens!" I yelled as I spiked the ball in the end zone.

The crowd was going wild. My teammates were thumping me on the back. I had done it!

"Nice going, Winters," Coach said, patting me on the shoulder as I returned to the bench. "I think the scout's going to like what he sees."

I played like a wild man for the rest of the game. Afterward Coach came up to me with a tall guy in a leather jacket. The guy handed me his card and said he'd like to invite me to come check out his school.

"Way to go, Winters," Wayne said, thumping me so hard, he nearly knocked me over. "A future Colorado State man. Not too shabby! Maybe we'll have Nebraska here next week and Notre Dame the week after, and then you can choose."

I felt myself smiling. It was something my face hadn't done in a while. "Yeah, how about that," I said.

"Listen, Rich," Wayne went on. "A group of us are getting together at my house before the home-coming dance. My dad's doing his famous barbecue.

You want to come? I know you weren't sure about going to the dance, but—"

"Sure. Great. Thanks, Wayne," I told him. "I'd love to come along. And I'm bringing Melanie."

Later that evening I walked outside to feed Sultan. He came over and nuzzled me with his big, soft nose.

"At least you're still glad to see me, guy," I said. Then it suddenly hit me—I didn't need to enter the rodeo anymore. I didn't need the money to go to New York. The smart thing would be to concentrate on my football and forget about everything else—and I meant *everything* else!

I finished feeding Sultan and decided I should go tell Melanie about my decision right away so that I didn't waste any more of her time.

I headed up to her house in the dark. It felt good to walk alone for a while in the cold night air.

Melanie came to the front door when I reached her house. "Hey, what's up?" she asked. "Nothing's wrong with Sultan, is it?"

"No, he's just fine," I said. "I came over to thank you for what you've done and to tell you that I won't be needing your help anymore."

"Really? You want to come in? It's kind of cold out here."

"Sure," I said, following her into the warm living room. I hadn't been in that room since Amber had moved out. It was weird to see new lamps, a new afghan over the sofa, and someone else's photos on the mantelpiece.

"Sit down," she said. "I'll make us hot chocolate if you like."

"That's okay. I'm not thirsty."

I took off my hat and sat on the big old sofa where I'd often sat with Amber. Melanie perched on the edge of Grandpa's rocking chair. It felt wrong to see her sitting there. Nobody but Grandpa ever sat in that chair before.

"So, why are you firing me as your horse trainer?" she asked quietly. "Is it something I've done?"

"Not at all," I told her. "You've been great. I never would've gotten Sultan into shape without you. It's just that you've wasted enough of your time with me. I'm not going to be entering any rodeos now."

"What? You're chickening out?"

"No. I don't need the money anymore," I explained. "Amber and I broke up."

"Oh, I see." She looked down at her hands. "Do you want to talk about it?"

"There's not much to tell," I said. "She's found herself a new guy. She said we both knew it was over. I sure as heck didn't, but apparently she did. Why else would she have kissed that jerk?"

"She told you she kissed another guy?"

I nodded.

"And that means it's over?"

"That makes it pretty definite, doesn't it? If you

kiss another guy, you must've gotten over the guy you left behind, right?"

"Not necessarily," Melanie said. "You do weird things when you're lonely and missing someone."

"You miss David, and you don't go around kissing everyone."

"Not yet. But if that creep doesn't show more interest soon . . ." She laughed to show she was making a joke. "But when you really love somebody," she continued in a more serious tone, "you don't give up so easily. True love's worth fighting for. At least, that's what I believe."

"How can I fight for her, huh?" I demanded. "She's two thousand miles away with some New York guy. She's surrounded by theater and museums and all sorts of things we don't have here. How can I possibly fight that?"

"Well, you could still win that rodeo prize money and buy a ticket to New York," she said. "You could show up there and sweep her off her feet."

"Yeah, right," I said, feeling hopeless. "You really think she'd want me back if I showed up?" I toyed with the fringe on the edge of my jacket. "It's not as simple as that, Melanie. There's another guy involved. *And* she thinks that there's something going on between you and me."

Melanie blinked back at me. "Between you and me?" she repeated.

"Some idiot told her I'd invited you to homecoming."

"You mean you hadn't told her?"

"No. Why do you sound so surprised? You said you weren't going to tell David."

Melanie shook her head. "I was just joking."

"Oh." I let out a heavy sigh. "Well, anyway, I didn't think she'd understand. I thought she'd get the wrong idea."

"Big mistake, Rich. How can you expect her to trust you if you keep things from her? No wonder she thought it was okay to date another guy. Call her up and set her straight."

I looked down at the floor. "It's too late now. She's already involved with someone else. She wouldn't want me back."

"Well, you can sit there feeling sorry for yourself if you like," Melanie said, "or you can fight for her. It's your choice, Rich. You're the only one who knows how much she means to you."

I glanced up. Melanie was sitting in the shadow, rocking in Grandpa's chair. For a moment the light played tricks on me. I could half imagine that Grandpa himself was sitting there. Suddenly I remembered that he'd said almost the same words before he left. I could hear his cracked old voice buzzing through my head right now, saying, *If you love her, fight for her.* Chills went up and down my spine.

I stood up and walked over to her. "Thanks a lot, Mel," I said, putting my hand on her shoulder. "You've made up my mind for me. I'm going to enter that rodeo, win a ton of money, and fly to New York. If this guy wants her, he's going to have to fight me for her!"

Thirteen

Amber

I WAS GLAD I was so busy that I didn't have time to miss Rich at all . . . well, hardly at all. When a siren would wake me up in the middle of the night, I'd lie there thinking about him, wondering if he was thinking about me. I'd picture him at that homecoming dance with Melanie. Did he hold her close, the way he'd held me? Did he look down into her eyes, smiling at her? And did he kiss her with the same passion and warmth that he'd kissed me so many times before?

But for the most part I barely had time to breathe, let alone think. Rehearsals went on until late every evening. There were costume fittings, and we all had to pitch in and help with building the set.

"Hi, there, stranger," Alicia said as I came into the cafeteria for the first time in a couple of weeks.

I'd been snatching sandwiches in between painting flats, but we'd finally finished up on the last backdrop the day before.

She patted the seat beside her. "I'd begun to think you'd flown right back to Wyoming."

An image of Rich popped into my head, and I almost replied, "I wish," but I swallowed the words back at the last minute. "You know what the last couple of weeks of rehearsals are like," I told her. "I feel like I'm living in that theater. Sean and I were saying that it might be a good idea to bring tents and sleeping bags and just not bother to go home anymore."

"That sounds cozy," Alicia commented, giving Mandy a knowing look as she and Suzanne sat down next to us. "A sleeping bag and Sean O'Brien?"

"Trust me—we'd be so tired, we'd fall asleep instantly," I said, feeling uncomfortable. I still felt wrong talking about my relationship with Sean, as if I was cheating on Rich somehow.

"I hear it's going great," Mandy said. "Suzanne says you're amazing."

"Thanks." I smiled. "It's a fun part to play. In fact, it would be hard to do it badly."

"Especially when Sean is your leading man in more ways than one," Suzanne said, nudging me. "You know, there are times I wonder why I was so excited to have you back here, Amber. You get the lead in the play and Sean too. Not fair!"

"Just be grateful that you don't have to stay at rehearsal until after ten every night," I told her.

"And have Sean walk me home?" she teased,

grinning at our other friends. "Ooh, that sounds really hard to take."

"You're a lucky girl, Amber." Mandy sighed.

"That's me—lucky," I said, nodding. Now all I had to do was believe it myself.

Sean is wonderful, I told myself. I was lucky to be dating him. If only I could make myself forget about Rich. . . .

It seemed like no time had passed before it was opening night. I was so nervous that I couldn't put on my own makeup—Suzanne had to do it for me.

"Relax, you're going to be great," she told me.

"It's just that this is the biggest thing I've ever done in my life," I said. "What if I forget my lines?"

"That's why they have a prompter," Suzanne said. "Besides, you won't forget them. You've said them a zillion times. You could say them in your sleep. All you have to do now is get out there and enjoy it. I know I'm going to."

"That's because you don't have to sing solos in front of all those people," I said, biting my lip. "What if I open my mouth and no sound comes out?"

Suzanne laughed. She grabbed my shoulders and shook me. "You are going to be an incredible success. Trust me. A great Broadway producer is going to be out there, and he's going to leap onto the stage when it's over, waving a contract at you."

I laughed. "My whole family is going to be out there, and that's bad enough." I sighed and stared at my reflection in the mirror. "I just wish my grandpa would've come," I said. "I asked him to. Dad offered to buy him a plane ticket and fly him out for the weekend, but he said he couldn't."

"Maybe he's scared of flying," Suzanne said. "Maybe his doctor won't let him. You know he'd come if he could."

I turned to smile at her. "Thanks, Suzanne. You're right. And you're a good friend. I'm sorry if I'm a pain sometimes." Out of nowhere I felt my eyes begin to well up with tears.

"What else are friends for?" she said. "Hey, don't cry. You're going to ruin your makeup."

There was a tap on the door, and one of the other girls went to open it. I heard her say, "You can't come in here, Sean. We're getting changed."

"I need to talk to Amber," he said.

I jumped up and ran to the door. "What's up?" I asked him.

He grinned. "I just wanted to say break a leg."

"You too." I smiled back at him.

"Well, I imagine you'll get lots of flowers tonight, so I decided on quality, not quantity," he said shyly. Then he handed me a box with one single, perfect, long-stemmed red rose placed in it.

Once again I felt like I was about to cry. "Sean, that is so sweet of you. I love it."

"Good. Anyway, I'd better get back to the dressing room, or I'll be in big trouble," he said. "See you onstage."

I nodded. "Okay."

"I can't kiss you, or I'll smudge your makeup,"

143

he said. He put his finger to his lips, then touched mine. "I'll save the real thing for the cast party—or make that after the cast party." He hurried back down the hallway.

I gazed down at the red rose as I carried it back into the dressing room. Sean had to be the sweetest guy in New York, I thought. As Mandy had said, I was very lucky.

So why was I hoping that Rich was miraculously in the audience?

As I stood in the wings, waiting for my first appearance onstage, I felt like my legs had turned to jelly. I was one big shiver. My mouth felt so dry that I was sure no sound would ever come out of it. Then the curtain went up. I stepped onto the stage and said my first words and completely forgot about being nervous.

My voice sounded a little shaky at the beginning of my first song, but pretty soon I was enjoying myself. When I said a funny line and the audience laughed, it felt exhilarating. And when Sean and I did our duet, we really had fun with it. His eyes sparkled as he looked at me.

It was all over in what seemed like minutes. Before I knew it, we were all standing in line, holding hands and taking a bow. When Sean and I stepped forward for our personal bow, he put my hand to his lips, then pushed me forward all on my own. I could see a sea of hands, applauding me. It was like a dream come true.

In the dressing room we were loud and silly,

giggling with hysterical relief. Lots of flowers arrived, including a beautiful arrangement from my parents. I was kind of disappointed that there was nothing from Grandpa. If he hadn't come, at least he could have sent me some flowers, couldn't he? But then, maybe they didn't do that kind of thing in Wyoming . . . although Rich definitely would have if we were still together. . . .

Stop thinking about Rich, I commanded myself. *Tonight is my night, and I'm going to enjoy it.*

After we'd changed back into our regular clothes and had taken off our makeup, we went to the music room, where there was an opening-night reception for the cast and their families. My family was waiting for me there.

"Amber, you were the best one!" Katie yelled as soon as she saw me.

They all pulled me into a hug.

"You were great, honey bun," Dad said. "How come I didn't know before what a talented daughter I have?"

"And you and Sean performed so well together." Mom beamed.

"I hated the mushy parts when you kissed," Beau told me. "The lassoing was cool, though."

Suddenly Sean was right by my side. "She throws a mean lasso," he said, slipping his hand into mine. "That's how she caught me."

At that moment Mr. Peters and the principal arrived with Mr. Tidesdale, who was grinning from ear to ear.

"Where is she?" Mr. Tidesdale boomed. "There she is. Amber, get over here. I want to shake your hand!"

After that it was lots more smiling and shaking hands. So many people were saying such nice things to me that it was almost too much to handle. Half an hour later my smile had begun to fade and I was looking longingly at the snack table when a red-haired man with a beard tapped my arm.

"So, Amber, where are you thinking of going to school next year?" he asked me.

"I haven't really decided yet," I said. "I've applied to a lot of schools."

"Well, I'm the head of drama at NYU," he said. "I hope you've already sent your application in to us. We give some good scholarships." He looked over at Sean. "You'll convince her, won't you, Sean? She couldn't do better, could she?"

"You know him?" I asked Sean in wonder as the man moved away.

"I did a summer program there," he explained. "I think that's where I want to go to school—they have great professors. And if Professor Barnard said that to you, that means you're in. Hey, how about that? Wouldn't it be cool if we went to the same school?"

I felt a great stab at my heart. It wasn't too long ago that I'd had this same conversation with Rich. Now we'd be going to schools in two different worlds and our paths would never cross again.

I've got to face reality, I told myself. *I've moved on. I've got a new life now. There's no going back. . . .*

I grabbed Sean's hand. "Come on, let's go attack that food table. I'm starving," I said quickly, dragging him across the room.

The play ran for four performances. Suddenly I was a big shot at school—everybody knew me.

Bailey stopped by my locker one day. "I hear you were quite a success as Annie Oakley," she said. "Now you've had your fifteen minutes of fame. The next play they do, everything will be back to normal, thank God."

"What do you mean by that?" I asked, narrowing my eyes at her.

"I mean next time we'll do a real play. Not some corny old relic from history. Too bad we're not going to do *Oklahoma!*, so you won't get another chance to star as the lovable hillbilly."

"You might be surprised, Bailey," I said, grabbing my books out of my locker. "I might be able to act as well as you can."

"Not a chance."

I shrugged. "Well, the head of drama at NYU thinks so. He wants me to go there next year. Oh, and Sean will be going with me. Maybe we'll see you there too?" With that, I gave her my brightest smile and walked away.

"Yes!" I said as soon as I reached the stairwell. A couple of months ago I'd been worried about surviving in New York City, and now I had it made. I was the star of the play, and I had a cute, sweet, sensitive boyfriend. What more could I want from life?

147

I headed down the stairs. Now if only I could make the empty feeling go away. . . .

On Saturday night Sean and I had time for a real date, our first since we'd gone into the final frenzy of rehearsals for the play.

He had bought tickets for a new off-Broadway play that all the critics had said was sensational. I found it very weird. The whole performance took place at a train station, and all the characters were waiting for a train that never came. Actors wandered onstage and off, pushing bicycles and muttering things that didn't make sense. I tried to get the gist of what was going on, but I couldn't. After a while I had the crazy desire to laugh. These people couldn't be taking themselves seriously, could they? This was a joke, right?

At one point an actor came to the front of the stage and announced, "I see the world as an orange. You take off the peel, suck out the juice, and then what's left? Just rotting peel, that's all."

I could almost hear Rich's voice whispering in my ear at that moment. "What a load of baloney," he'd say. "Did someone get paid to write this stuff?"

I grinned to myself and glanced at Sean. He was staring at the stage as if he was taking in every word. During a scene break he turned to me. "Good stuff, isn't it?" he whispered. "Very deep, huh?"

I blinked back at him. He liked this show?

What am I doing here? I found myself thinking. *I'd rather be out in the mountains than watching this garbage in a crowded city. This is not me.*

Rich's face swam before my eyes—Rich and I riding together with the wind in our faces, sitting together in the mountain meadow, watching the peaks turn red in the sunset. . . .

Suddenly I knew why the hollow emptiness inside me wouldn't go away. I still loved Rich. I'd always love Rich, even if I never saw him again.

After the show we stopped for a coffee at Fiorelli's. Sean was bursting with enthusiasm about the play. He didn't even seem to sense that I was out of sorts.

"Wasn't it different?" he asked. "I'd love to get a chance to be in something like that. Maybe at NYU, I will." He toyed with his coffee cup, then lifted his head and smiled at me. "You've sent in your application to NYU, right? Think of all the great love stories we could rehearse if we were there together—me as Romeo and you as Juliet? Nah, too corny. How about *A Streetcar Named Desire*? Blanche DuBois. Now, that's a meaty role. . . ."

He went on talking while I crumbled my biscotti into pieces. Sweet, cute Sean, I thought. What was there not to like about him? Everyone at school envied me. I should have been so happy. But I wasn't.

At that moment I knew that I couldn't go on living a lie any longer. I didn't love Sean. I'd never love Sean.

"What's up?" he asked, noticing my expression.

"You've been so great to me, Sean," I told him, fighting to get the words out. "This just isn't fair to you."

"What isn't?"

"That I'm still in love with Rich—that I think about him all the time when we're together."

Sean sighed. "It takes time to get over an old relationship," he said. "I understand that. But it's over, Amber. You have to let him go and get on with your life here."

"I know," I said, "but I can't—I don't think that true love comes around that often, Sean. And what Rich and I had was true love. It's not going to disappear that easily." I put my hand over his. "I know I'm very lucky to be dating you, and I probably should have my head examined for breaking up with you, but you deserve a girlfriend who can love you back. I'd never be more than a friend to you."

He nodded, looking down at the table. "That's one of the things I like about you. You're straight with people. You say what you think."

"It's an old Wyoming custom," I said, attempting to smile.

We walked home together in silence. I was upset, but I knew I had done the right thing.

Sean kissed me on the cheek before I went into my building.

"See ya around, I guess," he said. Then he turned up his collar against the wind and walked away into the night.

I expected to find everyone already in bed when I came upstairs—it was almost midnight. But most of the lights were still on, and my parents were sitting together in the living room. They looked up when I walked in.

"Wait a sec," I said, freezing in the doorway. "Did I do something wrong? You said my curfew was one o'clock, and it's not even—"

"Amber," my dad said, getting up from his chair. "We just got a phone call from Arizona. Your grandfather has passed away."

"Passed away?" I couldn't make sense of the words. I turned to my mother. "You mean Grandpa died?"

She nodded, her eyes red from crying. "Grandpa died."

Fourteen

Rich

I'D BEEN TO rodeos before, but always as a specta-tor. This was the first time I was in one competing, and I felt like a complete outsider. Everyone else seemed to know exactly what they were doing. They strolled into the registration booth, signed up, and strolled out again, saying hi to everyone they passed. Everyone knew everyone else—except me.

"I don't think this is the best idea after all," I muttered to Melanie. "I've changed my mind. I'll watch you compete, but I'm not entering."

"Rich, I didn't think you were a chicken," Melanie said. "I thought you had guts."

I flushed. "I do. I just hate making a fool of my-self, and that's what I'm going to do if I compete against these guys."

"So you're saying that Amber's not worth the

risk, right?" Melanie asked in a sugar-sweet voice.

I glared at her. "Of course she is."

Melanie shrugged. "If you want to see Amber and you need the prize money, you have to go for it. What's the worst thing that could happen? You lose, that's all."

"No, the worst thing that could happen is that Sultan runs off with me, I fall off, and I make a complete fool of myself," I said.

"That won't happen. You and Sultan are a team now. He won't let you down. Now quit worrying and go for it. And let me be for a while. I've got my own psyching up to do."

"Sorry," I said, embarrassed. I'd been so wrapped up in my own problems that I'd forgotten that Melanie had hers too.

I was only entering one event, the calf roping, and that didn't come until the end of the day. I sat there restlessly while I waited, watching the other contestants. They all knew their stuff, that was clear. Yup, I was definitely the only one who was likely to make a big fool of himself.

When it was finally our turn, Sultan sensed my nervousness and danced around when other horses came near him.

Just don't let me screw up big time, I prayed as I sat waiting for my turn in the arena.

I was one of the first to go. Before I knew it, the buzzer sounded and the calves came into the ring. I had my eye on a delicate little brown one— she'd have been easy to bring down. But Sultan had other ideas. With no help from me, he singled out a sturdy brown-and-white bull calf. We galloped alongside him, and the noose slipped easily over his head. The rope was around his feet before he knew what hit him. I had made a great time.

"Well, it wasn't pretty, but it sure was fast," Melanie said to me when I exited the ring.

"It was a total fluke," I muttered to her.

"Don't knock it. That time will probably stand."

Her prediction was true. More and more riders came and went, and my time was still the fastest. The guy who was last year's all-around champ was the last to enter the ring. He beat me by two-tenths of a second, and moved into first place.

I shook my head and let out a frustrated sigh.

"You got second," Melanie said, seeing my disappointment. "Second in your first rodeo? That's great, Rich."

"Yeah, sure."

"And you won a hundred dollars!"

"That will only get me as far as Chicago."

"So? It's a start, a good omen of things to come. You'll get the rest in time to go see Amber at Christmas." She nudged me. "Gotta go. I'm up for barrel racing. Wish me luck."

"Good luck," I said, giving her a smile. "Go get 'em, girl."

I went to the rail to cheer for her. Not that she needed my support—she was clearly the best, zipping around those barrels as if she and her horse were one fantastic creature.

Her face was glowing as she came out of the ring

and slid down from her horse. I ran over to her. "You were great, Mel. You were the best!" I yelled.

"That was awesome!" she exclaimed. She threw her arms around my neck, and we hugged. I picked her up and twirled her around. She was light as a feather. Her face was laughing up at me. Then I put her down, and she was standing there in my arms. I had a sudden crazy desire to kiss her.

"I, uh, think we'd better get these horses back to the trailer," she said, laughing nervously. "We've got a long drive ahead of us."

"Yeah. Good idea." I let her go and watched her as she walked away.

During the long drive home I had plenty of time to think. *Would that be such a bad idea, Melanie and me?* I wondered. We'd had a good time at the dance together—she'd been a lot of fun. And we had a lot in common. The only thing wrong with her was that she wasn't Amber. She would never be Amber.

Don't even go there, I told myself, focusing on the dark road ahead. *Don't even think about it. Melanie has David—she doesn't need you to complicate her life.* Also, I knew that it wouldn't be fair to Melanie to take things any further when I knew that I could never love her. All I wanted to do was go to New York and see Amber. And even if she didn't want me back, I'd never love anybody the way I loved her.

It was late when we finally arrived home, and I was beginning to notice the aches and pains that you get from wrestling a hefty bull calf. Melanie dropped me off at my place.

"Hey, the lights are still on," I said as I unloaded Sultan. "That's weird. They're usually asleep by this time. I hope nothing's wrong."

"They were probably just waiting for you to get back safely," Melanie said.

"Yeah, I bet you're right," I said. I grinned at her. "Well, thanks for everything, Melanie. You've been great. I wouldn't have—"

"Hey, cut that out," she interrupted, punching my arm. "If I hadn't have met you, I'd have been a basket case myself. And you did great today. Now we just have to work on your technique!"

"My technique?" I raised an eyebrow. "Now why would you think there's anything wrong with my technique?"

She laughed and honked as she drove away. I let Sultan into his corral and went into the house.

"It's okay; you can relax. Your little boy's home," I called to my parents as I walked in. "And you'll never guess what—" I broke off when I saw the serious expressions on their faces. "What? It's bad news, isn't it?"

My mom nodded and looked at my dad. "We just got a call from Arizona. Mr. Stevens died today," Mom said quietly.

"Amber's grandpa?" I shook my head in disbelief. "No. That can't be right. He was as strong as an ox."

"I'm sorry, Rich," Dad said, coming to put his hand on my shoulder. "I know how fond you were of him. It's a shock for us too. He was a great old man."

"And it turns out he wasn't as strong as an ox either," Mom told me. "He went to Arizona because his doctors had told him his heart wouldn't hold up much longer. He never told a soul about it except for his friend out there. He said he wanted to spare his family grief—that was just like him, wasn't it?"

I pressed my lips hard together and blinked back tears. I wasn't going to cry in front of them.

"The funeral's going to be here, on Thursday," Mom went on. "They're bringing his body to be buried in the churchyard, next to his wife."

"The funeral's going to be here?" I repeated. All this was just starting to sink in. "Will Amber's family be coming?"

"I'm sure they will," Mom said.

Amber! I was going to get my wish and see her again. But I hadn't imagined it would be for something like this. How could I even talk to her at her grandpa's funeral? I'd probably be the last person she'd want to see.

Of course, she'd be wrapped up in her own grief, I realized. She'd hardly notice whether I was there or not. I pictured us sitting in that little white church like two strangers, not saying a word to each other.

I didn't sleep much that night. Conflicting emotions were swirling around my head. The gnawing emptiness of grief for a man I thought of as a second grandfather fought with the excitement and despair of seeing Amber again.

The next morning I was up at dawn. It had rained during the night, and the peaks to the west were dazzling white with a fresh coating of snow. I got dressed and walked outside, realizing after a few steps that I should have put on my heavy jacket, but I didn't really care. The wind stung my cheeks and ears, but I didn't care about that either.

I walked and walked aimlessly, not paying attention to where I was going. But before long I looked up and saw that I was standing outside the gate to the Stevenses' place.

Now it would never be the Stevenses' place again, I thought. It would be sold, and strangers would move in. Maybe Melanie's family would buy it, but it still would never be the same. I'd never stop by there on a summer evening and sit on the porch, sharing a lemonade with the old man. I'd never help him with his hay making or ranching again.

And Amber wouldn't have any reason to come back here in the summer.

My whole body shook with a big sigh. I glanced up when I heard footsteps on the gravel driveway. Melanie was coming toward me.

"Hi," she said. "You can come in if you like. You don't have to stand outside the gate. The dogs won't bite."

"Thanks, but I wasn't really coming to see you. I was just walking, and I wound up here."

"I understand. I heard about Mr. Stevens. I'm sorry. It must've been a shock for you."

I nodded. "He was like my own grandfather." I looked down at my hands. "You know, Amber's coming back here for the funeral. I don't think I'll go. I couldn't handle it."

"Not go?" Melanie squeezed my arm. "Of course you have to go, Rich. You owe it to Mr. Stevens, don't you?"

"Yes, but—"

"And all you ever talk about is seeing Amber again."

I shook my head. "Yes, but—"

"But what?" she demanded, her hands on her hips. "You don't really want to see her again after all?"

"Of course I do, but not like this. I won't know what to say, Mel. And I know I'll cry and make a fool of myself."

"You have to go anyway," Melanie said firmly. "Everyone will expect you to be there. *Amber* will expect you to be there. You have to go whether you like it or not."

I took a deep breath and thought for a moment. "How come you're always right?" I asked her at last.

She grinned. "Just born that way, I guess."

Somehow I made it through until Thursday. I heard that Amber's family was flying in on Wednesday night and staying at the Cowboy Village Motel about a mile out of town. I stayed home on Wednesday night and thought out what I would say to Amber.

I'm really sorry to hear about your grandpa. He was a wonderful man. I couldn't go wrong with that, could I? But should I just leave it at that or let her know how much I'd been missing her? Should I set her straight about Melanie and me? Should I drop a hint that I'd been planning a surprise visit?

Any words that I tried to come up with sounded corny. I decided that the best thing to do would be to see how she reacted to me and take it from there. Surely I'd know if that old spark was still there. If it was, then everything else would come naturally.

On Thursday morning I woke up and put on my good dark suit. My stomach was churning nervously—I couldn't touch the pancakes and bacon that my mom put in front of me. It was hard enough to swallow the cup of coffee.

In an hour I'm going to see her, I told myself. Then I reminded myself that in an hour I was also going to help put Mr. Stevens to rest. That was the main purpose of today, and I'd better not forget it.

Just before we were due to leave for the church, Melanie showed up at our front door. She looked very different from usual in a long black dress and jacket. Her hair was sleeked back into a bun, making her appear elegant and much older. I stepped outside to talk to her.

"I just wanted to let you know that I'd see to your horses after the funeral so that you don't have that chore today. I imagine you won't feel like doing much," she said quietly.

I gave her a small smile, feeling very grateful to have such a great friend. "Thanks, Mel."

"Hang in there, cowboy. You can handle this," she said, then hugged me. I wrapped my arms around her and hugged her back.

I sensed, rather than heard, that someone else was watching us. I looked over the top of Melanie's head to see Amber staring at me. My whole body tensed up, suddenly frozen, but my mind started racing. I had to let Amber know this wasn't what she thought!

Fifteen

Amber

ALL THE WAY to Wyoming, I had psyched myself up for the moment when I'd see Rich again. *When we look at each other, we'll know that everything's going to be all right,* I thought.

I'd chanted this to myself over and over as I walked up the road from the church to Rich's house. I had to see him before the service. I needed to see him to get through this.

And there he was, standing with his arms around some girl. Her head was against his chest, and they looked like they belonged together. I wanted to slip away without their seeing me, but at the last second Rich glanced up. Our eyes met.

I didn't wait a moment longer. I turned, running back down the driveway as fast as I could in my black patent leather shoes. I heard him yelling, "Amber, wait," but I didn't stop.

I didn't slow down until I joined my parents outside the church.

"Oh, there you are, honey," Mom said. "The hearse should be arriving any moment now."

The hearse—with my grandpa's coffin in it. Tears stung my eyes. How was I going to get through this? How could I even bear to look at that wooden casket with his body inside it?

Grandpa! I thought. *If only I could've said good-bye to you. If only I could've hugged you one more time and told you how much I love you.*

I swallowed back the big lump in my throat and moved away from my family so that I didn't have to talk to anyone. I started to walk through the thick carpet of fallen leaves, standing alone by the row of tall pine trees that encircled and protected the little white church. It was so peaceful here. Behind the church the hills rose, tier after tier fading into blue distance where the peaks were sparkling with snow. I'd forgotten how beautiful this all was, how good and fresh the air was, how much I missed it all.

When I'd first heard the news about Grandpa, I'd been in a total state of shock. I had never expected that to happen in a million years. Grandpa was a strong guy. I thought he was going to live to be a hundred. I was completely out of it as I packed my bag and called my friends, and it wasn't until I was sitting on the plane with time to think that it hit me—I was going to see Rich again. That thought spread like a warm glow through my frozen body.

All through the long plane ride and the drive that followed, I'd pictured the moment when we met again. He might've been dating Melanie, but he couldn't love her, not the way he'd loved me. I would set him straight about Sean and me, and we'd laugh over our dumb misunderstandings. Then everything would be perfect between us again.

Now I shook my head angrily, fighting to hold back the tears that were crowding my eyes. How dumb I had been to think that everything would be perfect when I saw Rich again. I shut my eyes to try to blot out that painful image of seeing Rich's arms around Melanie. I didn't know it was possible to feel so much pain and despair—the double pain of losing my grandfather and now losing Rich for a second time.

There was a deep, nagging pain in my chest that wouldn't go away. My heart truly felt like it was breaking.

"Come on, Amber. We're going in now." Dad tapped my arm, and I followed him into the church, moving mechanically like a robot. We had to sit in the front pew with Grandpa's coffin, hidden under a mountain of flowers, right in front of us. I wanted to turn around to see if Rich was there, but I didn't. If he'd been sitting with Melanie, holding her hand, it would've been more than I could bear.

The service seemed to go on and on. People stood up to speak about Grandpa. My father spoke last of all, saying how glad he was that he got to know his father before he died. They'd been apart for so many years. If we hadn't come back to live in Wyoming, they'd never have become friends. He didn't break down in the middle, as I know I would've done. I was proud of him—it must have been so hard. It was hard enough for me just sitting there.

Finally the organ played "Amazing Grace." Dad and Beau went to escort Grandpa's coffin out of church. Mom, Katie, and I followed. Katie slipped her hand into mine. I passed a blur of faces, but I didn't notice Rich.

We stepped outside, and suddenly I knew that I couldn't go to the graveyard and watch Grandpa be lowered into the ground. And I couldn't face all my former friends and neighbors at the reception afterward. It was just too much.

I let go of Katie's hand. "I'll see you guys in a while," I whispered, then slipped away from the procession.

I started walking fast. I had no idea where I was going—I just wanted to be alone and far away. An icy wind was blowing, and it cut right through my flimsy clothes, snatching away my breath. Clouds had moved in, hiding the sun and blocking out the mountains. Any minute now it was going to snow.

I kept on walking until I found myself at the gate to Grandpa's old house. Our old house. Nothing had changed since I'd left. I stood staring at it, half expecting Grandpa to appear on the porch and yell to me, "Don't just stand there, child.

There's chores waiting to be done. I need you to go up to the top pasture with me."

"I'll come with you, Grandpa," I whispered. "Anywhere you want to go is fine with me."

I took in every detail of the house—especially the porch where we used to sit on hot summer evenings, drinking Grandpa's homemade lemonade. I pictured Rich and me, sitting together on the porch swing, my head on his shoulder, watching the fireflies on warm June nights. There was my window. How often I'd looked out it when I'd heard Rich's truck coming for me. And there was the old tractor that I'd had to drive during a snowstorm. There had been some scary times here and a lot of hard work too. But at least we'd known that we were alive, every single day. And there had been some wonderful times too.

Now it would never be my home again. I'd have no excuse to come here in the summer. I'd never see Rich again—he was a part of every single memory about this place. He had been the most important part of my life for so long. And tomorrow I'd get on a plane and never see him again.

I closed my eyes and remembered how he looked when he'd swing himself down from his truck and walk toward me, tipping back that black cowboy hat and letting his light brown hair spill across his forehead. And a little half smile would cross his face, and his blue eyes would light up. . . . It was too painful to bear. I opened my eyes.

Rich was standing a few yards away, watching me.

For a second I thought I was hallucinating. Then he spoke.

"Are you okay?" he asked.

I nodded, my breath catching in my throat.

"Nobody knew where you went," he said. "They were worried. I guessed you'd be here."

"I couldn't face all those people at the reception." I fought to keep my voice even. "And I couldn't go without taking a last look at this place."

"A lot of memories here, huh?" he said. "For me too. It's hard to think that he's gone, isn't it?"

"I didn't get to say good-bye, Rich," I blurted out. "I didn't get to tell him how much I loved him. Why didn't I write more? Why didn't I call him more often? If only I'd known he was sick . . ."

"Nobody knew," he said. "And that's the way he wanted it. He was a proud man, Amber. The last thing in the world he'd have wanted was people fussing over him."

We stood there quietly for a long moment, just staring at each other. "Thanks for coming to check on me," I said finally. "Will you tell them I'll be back in a little while?"

"Do you want me to stay with you?"

"It's okay—you don't have to. I'll be fine. I just want to say my good-byes to the house. I don't suppose I'll ever see it again."

"No, I don't suppose so," Rich said. "You're heading straight back to New York, then?"

"Tomorrow," I told him. "I go home tomorrow."

He nodded. "Then I guess I won't see you again."

I have to see you again, I thought desperately as I looked into his eyes. But aloud I said, "I guess not."

"Well," he said. "I should be getting back. I promised my mom I'd help hand around food at the reception."

He looked at me long and hard, then turned to walk away.

Say something! a voice in my head screamed. *Don't let him go like that. Don't let him walk out of your life forever. . . .*

I opened my mouth. It was hard to speak. The winter wind snatched at my words as I forced them out.

"Rich!" I yelled at last.

He stopped and turned to look at me.

"Don't go," I said.

Sixteen

Rich

S HE WAS STANDING there, her copper-colored hair and her black silky scarf blowing out in the wind, looking at me with big, frightened eyes. She looked fragile enough to be blown away. I'd never seen her look prettier or sadder.

Leave right now while you have time, before you get yourself hurt again, a warning voice in my head was saying. *She only wants you here because she's grieving for her grandfather.*

But I couldn't leave.

I started to walk back toward her. I longed to rush up to her and wrap her tightly in my arms and tell her that everything was going to be all right, but I forced myself to stay cool.

"You'll freeze if you go on standing here like that. Do you want to take a walk?" I asked.

She nodded. "Okay."

We set off down the path, side by side, with great drifts of dead leaves swirling around us in the fierce wind. We passed the back of the barn and walked between the fields. There were no cattle in them now—they were deserted and empty. I looked over at what had been a lush pasture down by the creek, where Mr. Stevens had kept his prize bull. A memory came rushing back to me—Katie had wandered into that field to pet Old Barnaby once, not knowing that bulls could be dangerous. Amber had gone in to rescue her, nearly getting killed herself. And I'd yelled at Amber because I thought she didn't know any better. She'd yelled right back at me. It was the moment I'd fallen in love with her, I guess.

"Hey, do you remember when you first got here and your little sister got into that field with the bull?"

For a brief second a smile lit up her eyes. "She wanted to pat the nice cow," Amber said. "You saved her."

"So did you," I said. "In fact, you always were pretty gutsy. That's one of the things I've always liked about you. You never give up on things."

"I feel like giving up now," Amber said. "I just don't know how to handle this, Rich."

"I know it's hard, but your grandpa had to die sometime. Everyone has to die sometime."

"But there are so many things I wish I'd done, so many things I wanted to tell him."

"I think he knew most of those things," I told her. "He was a pretty sharp guy, your grandpa. And

I think he knew he wouldn't be coming back here. He talked to me about you before he left."

"He did? What did he say?"

"He said I should keep an eye on you and not let you get too caught up in New York."

She smiled. "Anything else?"

"Yeah." I took a deep breath, preparing myself to say the words I needed to say to her. "He said I shouldn't let you slip away, that I should be prepared to fight for you. I was going to follow that advice, Amber. I'd made up my mind to get a plane ticket to New York and make that jerk fight me for you."

Amber looked at me and laughed. "You were really planning to do that?"

I nodded. "This winter vacation. I've already won some of the money in a rodeo. I came in second in the calf roping."

"Second in the rodeo, huh? I thought I told you not to mess with rodeos—they're too dangerous." She was looking away, so I couldn't see her expression. Then she said quietly, "You wouldn't have to fight for me, you know. It would be no contest."

My heart pounded. "Meaning what? That he'd whup me or I'd whup him?"

"Neither. Meaning that there never was a question for me. I was never in love with Sean."

Relief flooded my body. "But you kissed him. You told me."

"One little kiss, Rich. It just sort of happened. It didn't mean that I'd fallen in love with him."

I was still not convinced. It seemed too good to be true. "But you're dating him."

"And you're not dating Melanie?" Now she turned to face me, her hands on her hips.

"No, I'm not, actually," I said.

"Oh, sure. I believe that. You took her to your homecoming dance. And I saw you in each other's arms today."

"For your information, Melanie was giving me a friendly hug because she knew today would be hard for me. She knew how fond I was of your grandfather and how worked up I was about seeing you again."

Amber didn't say anything, so I continued. "And I took her to the dance because I really didn't want to miss out on it my senior year. She didn't have anyone to go with either because she left her boyfriend back in Denver and she was really missing him."

"Oh," Amber said, turning away again and resting her hands on a fence post.

"So you see," I went on. "I wasn't the one who broke our promise and started dating someone else."

"I broke up with him, Rich," she said quietly. "I told him I could never love him because I was still in love with you. So I broke up with him, even though I thought I had lost you forever."

I put my hands on her shoulders. "I thought I'd lost you forever," I said, shuddering with emotion. "I've never been more miserable in my life."

"Oh, Rich," Amber said, then threw herself into my arms. "We've both been such idiots, haven't we?"

"Speak for yourself," I said shakily.

"You were just as big an idiot as I was—admit it," Amber said, her eyes laughing up into mine. "You were jealous because I was spending so much time doing other things, just like I was jealous of the time you were spending with Melanie."

"I guess we weren't too good at trusting each other after all."

"Long-distance romances are hard," Amber said. "You start imagining all kinds of dumb things."

"Tell me about it." I laughed and hugged her tight.

"I'm not long-distance right now, Rich," she said softly. "I'm right here, and nobody's watching." She stood on her toes to reach my face.

Her lips were cold when they met mine, but they warmed up right away. It was the moment I had dreamed about and imagined for so long. And it was just as good as it was in my dreams—better, in fact. I didn't want that kiss ever to end.

"Oh, Rich," she whispered as we finally drew apart. "I didn't think I'd ever feel happy again. I thought I'd lost Grandpa and I'd lost you too."

"And it was your grandpa who brought us together again," I said. "If you hadn't had to come back here, who knows if I'd have gotten up the nerve to go to New York."

"Would you really have challenged Sean to a fight?" Her eyes were teasing mine.

I nodded. "Absolutely."

"That's not very civilized, you know. It's not the way we go about things in the big city."

"I'm a simple country boy," I said, squeezing

172

her tightly. "I'm prepared to fight for my woman if I have to."

"Well, you don't have to," she said, kissing me again.

At that moment the sun broke through the thick layer of clouds, bathing us in golden light.

We stood there for a long moment, just smiling at each other in the sunlight.

"Promise me one thing," I said at last. "Promise me that we'll never doubt each other again. If you want to act in plays, fly to Paris, whatever, it's all right with me."

"I promise," Amber said, nodding. "And if you want to ride in rodeos, it's all right with me—as long as you don't try any of the dangerous stuff, like bronc riding."

"I promise. No bronc riding," I agreed.

"I guess we'd better be getting back," Amber said, untangling herself from my arms. "They'll all be wondering where we went."

"And my mom will be mad that I'm not handing around her stuffed chili peppers."

"Stuffed chili peppers? Let's go," she said, pulling me along. "Suddenly I'm starving. I don't think I've eaten a thing for weeks."

"Me neither," I said. I grinned at her. "I'll race you back there."

We took off, laughing and jostling each other down the narrow track. If anyone had seen us, they wouldn't have thought it was proper behavior for the day of a funeral. But I knew that Amber's grandpa would have thought it was just fine.

Seventeen

Amber

BEFORE WE GOT back to the community center, where the funeral reception was being held, it started to snow—a few flakes at first, but then harder and harder. By the time we reached the building, it was coming down as hard as ever.

"There you are," my mother said, rushing up to me as we came through the door. "We were so worried about you."

"Mom thought you'd gone to throw yourself off a high cliff," Beau said with a delighted smile. "Then she thought that you'd be lost in the blizzard and freeze to death in the snow. She was about to send out search parties."

"I knew you'd be okay," Katie said, wrapping her arms around my snowy legs. "I knew Rich had gone to find you, and he wouldn't let anything bad happen to you."

"Smart kid," Rich said, ruffling her hair. "You're right. I won't let anything bad happen to her, ever."

I felt a wonderful warm glow in my heart as he smiled at me.

"Look at you two," Rich's mom said, coming over to us with a tray of food. "Fancy letting her walk through the snow in those clothes, Rich. You take her back to the house this instant. Run her a good hot bath and then find her some warm clothes, or we'll have a case of pneumonia on our hands."

I didn't need to be told twice. I hadn't even felt the cold until that moment—I was too happy, I guess. But now I'd started to shiver again. I let Rich take me back to his house, and soon I was soaking in the luxury of a big old claw-foot tub.

Rich's mom arrived just after I'd dried off and put on one of Rich's big sweaters. "We sent everyone home," she said. "We didn't want anyone stranded with all that snow coming down."

Rich looked out the window. "Looks pretty bad," he said. "In fact, you might not be able to get back to New York tomorrow. You might just find yourself snowed in for the whole winter."

"Okay with me," I said, smiling at him.

"You could stay here all year," he went on. Then his face grew serious. "Why don't you? I could build you a spare room out in the barn. Or maybe you could board with Melanie at your grandpa's house. I know they've got rooms to spare. We could finish high school together, just like we wanted."

I was tempted. Boy, was I tempted. But I shook my head. "I have to go back, Rich. I like my school. I'm in great classes that will help me get into a good college next year."

He made a face. "A good college, as in East Coast? Ivy League?"

"Not necessarily," I said. "Actually, I don't think I want to be stuck in a big city. Being back here has reminded me how much I love the freedom of the wide-open spaces. I don't think I'm a city girl at heart."

Rich grinned. "Well, Colorado has some good schools."

"I know it does. University of Colorado. Colorado State . . ."

"To which I might be going next year," he said.

My heart rose. "Really?"

He nodded. "They might offer me a scholarship."

"Rich, that's wonderful!"

"I haven't totally decided yet," he said. "Other schools might offer me something better. I'll need more information before I can make up my mind."

"About their academic programs?"

He smiled and shook his head. "About which school you want to go to. I'm not going through this again. I'm sticking to you like glue from now on, Amber Stevens."

I smiled back at him, relieved. "That's just fine with me."

*   *   *

That evening Rich's mom had my parents over for dinner. We sat around in Rich's big, warm kitchen and talked and laughed a lot. It was as if all the sadness of the morning had been washed away. Of course we all missed my grandpa, but he would want us to laugh and enjoy life.

We were in the middle of washing up when there was a knock at the door. Rich's dad went to get it, and we heard him say, "Go right on in."

A girl burst into the room. Her hair was flying every which way, and her cheeks were bright red from the wind. She was wearing riding clothes, and it didn't take a genius to realize that this was the famous Melanie.

She ran right up to Rich. "I had to come right over and share the news with you," she said, beaming. "I'm so happy, I could kiss you."

Rich shot me a worried look. "Uh—Amber's here with her family, Mel," he said.

Melanie turned to me with a big smile. "Wow, I'm so happy to finally meet you, Amber! I'm sorry about your grandfather."

"Thanks," I said.

After Rich introduced her to my parents, Melanie looked around and noticed the remains of dinner still on the table. "Sorry to barge in like this," she said to all of us, "but I just had to tell Rich my good news."

"What is it?" he asked.

"It's David," she said. "I wrote to him and told him I wasn't going to play second fiddle in his life anymore. It was all or nothing with me. If he couldn't be bothered to take the time to see me, then it was over."

"Wow," Rich said. "And what happened?"

"He called tonight. He just got the letter, and he's scared silly. He's coming up here next weekend, and I've been invited to spend Christmas with his parents. I'm so excited!"

"That's great, Mel," Rich said, grinning. "I'm glad things worked out well for both of us."

Melanie turned to me again. "David's my boyfriend," she said. "I had to leave him back in Colorado." She sighed. "Long-distance relationships aren't easy. It's hard when you can't actually see the person."

"Tell me about it," Rich said, smiling at me.

"Oh, well, gotta go," Melanie said. "Have a good flight home, Amber. Be seeing you, I'm sure."

"I hope so," I told her.

"By the way, we really like the house," Melanie said. "My dad was wondering whether you guys are going to sell the place now that your grandpa's gone."

I felt a big surge of panic. Sell the place? What were we going to do?

But before I could say anything, my dad spoke. "No, Melanie. We won't be selling the house. I plan to keep it just the way it is and come spend our summers out here. And who knows, someday . . ." His gaze wandered to Rich and me.

I felt a tide of happiness wash over me. Summers in Wyoming. My grandpa's house waiting for me whenever I wanted it. And someday maybe Rich and I would come to live in that house, just like my grandpa wanted. . . . What a wonderful future lay ahead of me.

I couldn't wait for it to start.

Do you ever wonder about falling in love? About members of the opposite sex? Do you need a little friendly advice but have no one to turn to? Well, that's where we come in . . . Jenny and Jake. Send us those questions you're dying to ask, and we'll give you the straight scoop on life and love.

DEAR JAKE

Q: *I've been friends with Jonah for a while, but lately I've started to want more than a friendship. Now whenever we hang out together, I get so nervous, I can't talk to him. I feel like I'm making a fool of myself, and I'm sure he thinks so too. What's going on?*

MD, Van Nuys, CA

A: First of all, remember that Jonah's just a guy. Although we often act like nothing can shake up our perfectly cool selves, the truth is, inside we get as nervous about things as girls do. In all likelihood, if Jonah's noticed the change in your behavior, he's probably wondering what *he's* done wrong.

Before you can reach a point where you're comfortable sharing your new feelings with Jonah, you need to take a few steps. One good way to ease into a comfort zone with him is to get used to interaction in a group setting. Once you see how easy it is to chat with Jonah when others are around, you'll find that one-on-one isn't nearly as intimidating. Also, you'll remember that this is the same guy who you used to feel totally normal around and the only thing that's changed is how you feel about him.

Q: *Bob has been a friend of mine for almost three years, and he's had a serious girlfriend the whole time. I'm not a relationship wrecker, so I never told Bob that I have a huge crush on him myself. The thing is, he and his girlfriend broke up a few weeks ago. He still seems really sad, and I want to finally tell him how I feel, but I'm not sure about timing. How long should I wait before I let him know? And how do I break the news when the time comes?*

LA, Uvalde, TX

A: Three years is a considerable chunk of a person's life, and breaking up with somebody after that long can be really difficult. You're definitely right to hesitate. The timetable on this stuff is a totally individual thing, so I can't tell you exactly when to drop your bombshell. It's not so much a quantity thing as a quality one—let him get to the point where every other word in his mopey monologues isn't his ex's name, and watch him for signs of renewed enthusiasm about the world around him.

Bob's finally coming back to planet Earth? Okay, so when you decide to tell him, tread carefully. Casually bring up the topic of dating in conversation, and judge his reaction. If he still seems awkward with the idea of going out with someone, hold off a little longer. At this point any girl he dates will be the rebound girl, and you do *not* want to be rebound girl. Rebound relationships are usually just a quick solution and rarely, if ever, last. Instead be the friend who helps him through his pain and then the girl who's there when he's ready to love again.

DEAR JENNY

Q: *Mary and I have been best friends our whole lives, but lately our friendship has become so strained. I've had a few crushes on guys I know, and whenever I want to talk about them, she immediately changes the topic. She also gets upset if I invite any guys out with us. What should I do?*

KS, Winchester, MA

A: It sounds like you and your friend have reached a point where your interests and tastes are dividing. This is common between people who have been close for an extended time since it's natural to change over the years and you won't always change in the same ways that your friend does.

Your newfound interest in guys is normal, but it's possible that Mary hasn't reached that point yet and resents the feeling of being left behind as you move on. Try talking to her about the problem—tell her your feelings and let her explain hers. It could help to remind her how special she is to you and how much you value having her there as a sounding board for all the parts of your life, including your crush updates. If you're still hoping to preserve this friendship, see if you can work out a compromise. Agree to make your time with Mary boy-free, but make it clear that you want to spend other nights hanging out with your guy friends.

Do you have questions about love? Write to:
Jenny Burgess or Jake Korman
c/o 17th Street Productions,
a division of Daniel Weiss Associates, Inc.
33 West 17th Street
New York, NY 10011

Don't miss any of the books in *Love Stories*
—the romantic series from Bantam Books!